THE ARMY WITHIN ZHANLUE
(STRATEGY)

Jack D. Waggoner

Author's Tranquility Press
ATLANTA, GEORGIA

Copyright © 2024 by Jack D. Waggoner

All rights reserved. No part of this publication may be reproduced, distributed or transmitted in any form or by any means, including photocopying, recording, or other electronic or mechanical methods, without the prior written permission of the publisher, except in the case of brief quotations embodied in critical reviews and certain other noncommercial uses permitted by copyright law. For permission requests, write to the publisher, addressed "Attention: Permissions Coordinator," at the address below.

Jack D. Waggoner/Author's Tranquility Press
3900 N Commerce Dr. Suite 300 #1255
Atlanta, GA 30344, USA
www.authorstranquilitypress.com

Ordering Information:
Quantity sales. Special discounts are available on quantity purchases by corporations, associations, and others. For details, contact the "Special Sales Department" at the address above.

Copyright Registration No. TXu 2-451-972
Effective Date: September 13, 2024

The Army Within Zhanlue / Jack D. Waggoner
Hardback: 978-1-966088-49-3
Paperback: 978-1-965463-96-3
eBook: 978-1-965463-16-1

Reader Information:

Author note: The reader can follow the process started in 1998 by reading:

BIRD NEST

Library of Congress No. 2008934628

Dorrance Publishing Co. Inc. 1-800-788-7654

ISBN: 978-1-4349-0165-1

THE RAINBOW ZHANLUE (Strategy)

Library of Congress No. 2011961184

Xlibris Publishing - 844-714-8691

ISBN: Hardcover 978-1-4653-0837-5

Softcover 978-1-4653-0836-8

E-book 978-1-4653-0838-2

DRAGON BREATH ZHANLUE (Strategy)

Library of Congress No. 2022917682

Author Reputation Press - 888-821-0229

ISBN: Softcover 979-8-88514-399-8

E-book 979-8-88514-398-1

CHAPTER ONE

Jet How Chueng, the President of China's, long time comrade and trusted hatchet-man, for the past thirty years, set quietly in the Presidents underground garden watching two majestic swans meander their way across a sparkling pond. A multi-level waterfall provided a misty backdrop and the smell of tropical vegetation permeated the air.

It truly was a tranquil setting, both sight and sound, and Jet smiled as he recalled all the important decisions, world altering decisions and strategies (zhanlues) that had been hatched, refined and implemented from this underground world.

The current zhanlue, nearing the end of its refinement, would cement China's domination of the world and was by far the most ambitious zhanlue ever undertaken by any country in world history; yes, even more ambitious than Romes grand design to control the known world before Christ was born.

The Cheshire cat smile that President Hu's comrade flashed was diabolical and was not just an idea, wondering around an old man's head, but a reality that had been operational for over three years, ever since the election of Joseph Robinette Biden Jr. as the forty-six President of the United States of America.

Jet was extremely proud of the work he had done prior to the American election of 2020 and the 100 million U.S. dollars that President Hu had deposited in his bank account was ample proof that his efforts had been appreciated.

Over his shoulder Jet heard a familiar voice and at once rose, turned, and greeted the General Secretary of the CPC, central committee which was President Hu's official title.

"Comrade Jet, come set with me inside. We have a lot to discuss and I have missed you. How are you enjoying your new home on Bai'an Island?"

"It is coming together and my sister in-law and her family seem to be enjoying themselves with all the activities of installing the family in new quarters. Took us almost two years to get the house and grounds finished and now everyone is working on the furnishings. Nothing but antiques will do so we should really be shopping at the national museum."

"After we take Taiwan, I will let you have your pick from all the items they stolen from us when they fled to their island fortress. I understand they have enough treasure that the multilevel museum, outside Taipei rotates the collection every five years and there are still items that have never seen the light of day."

"That is something to look forward to Comrade," Jet replied.

Jet added, "Since I am no longer in your daily loop will that happen before Biden's term comes to an end?"

President Hu smiled at Jet and mouthed a big 'YES' with no sound, but flashing eyes.

Jet smiled to himself and the memories flashing through his brain saw a young Colonel, ushered into the Supreme Generals office and an intimidating voice demanding, "Colonel, go to Tienanmen Square and stop the protests, by any means necessary. End it in the next twelve hours and if any superior questions your resolve refer them to me. Understood?"

Sweat beads popped out on Jets forehead just remembering the day and his resulting actions.

President Hu looked at the man setting across from him and casually asked, "Are you remembering the first day we met?"

Jet nodded yes and President Hu continued. "That decision and that day defined my power and your performance exceed all my expectations and ever request, since then, has convinced me that without you this administration might just be a footnote in Chinese history. I am indebted to you and I value your friendship above all others, including my beautiful wife."

"Thank you, Comrade, and for the record it has been one hell of a ride!"

Both men laughed and the mutual admiration darts flashed across the room.

"Jet, the zhanlue we developed just before your retirement has been working without hardly any daily hands-on direction thanks to our greedy friend in the White-house and his endless selection of the worst-case actions. For example we now have almost two hundred billion in American machinery and weapons that they left in Afghanistan and it cost us almost nothing as the Taliban leaders knew it would turn into a pile of rust if left to their people to study. It's just been a roller coaster of a ride with Joe in charge and it has given us a real leg up on future military planning and development."

"That's good news indeed Comrade but how does that work not having a direct responsible party other than you, of course?"

"I am glad you asked. I want your opinion on the person that I have selected to ramrod this zhanlue, to its ultimate conclusion, once we have taken the necessary steps to neutralize the Taiwan situation and that is behind us." Looking at Jet with the black eyes sparkling he continued, "We want to strike, with the new zhanlue as quickly as Taiwan is secure. They won't be expecting that and surprise will defiantly give us the edge."

Jet leaned in and asked, "Is your selected operative already on station?"

"Yes, he is posing as the CEO of a new battery plant being built in Manteno, Illinois." Then with a grin that would light up half of Asia he continued, "It's costing us 2 billion US dollars but when we take over the country it will just be another asset, among hundreds of thousands of others."

Pausing and looking right through Jet with a cold eye stare he continued, "They allow us to buy their wheat land, to gobble up their pharmaceutical industries and end up thanking us. It's truly mind boggling that their leadership is so brain dead, don't you agree?"

"Yes, I watched the last three years and its almost like Biden wants to shoot himself in the foot so he can limp all the way to the bank, with our money while the American public tries to cope with inflation, crime immigration pollution and shrinking food supplies."

"Jet, do you think it will be an easy or difficult sale to convince the American people that China can better lead them than their current leadership?"

Jet smiled and said, "Follow the food.... If we control the food, we control the population. We can let millions of them die; after all there are millions of our loyal comrades that would gladly trade their Beijing apartment for a farm in Iowa, in a heartbeat. Don't you think?"

President Hu nodded agreement and added, "I have chosen Lin Wong."

Jet cocked his head, looked at his supreme leader and nodded his agreement. "A bold choice. Yes, very bold but I recall meeting with him in Hawaii and he has qualities that you don't find in the average military/bureaucrat type. Put him on a short leash Comrade and I'm sure you will look back with no regrets. Power is corrupting and you know he will end up being the most powerful person in the party, other than yourself, of course."

"Yes, I understand where you're coming from but his second in command is on my personnel payroll and we have an understanding that if there needs to be an accident he will so arrange and he is being paid a princely sum to stand ready should I feel that Lin is getting out of control or too big for his britches."

Jet nodded agreement and concluded, "Well Comrade it would appear that you have this zhanlue under control. Do you have any specific time table set up yet?"

"Yes, after Taiwan has fallen, very quickly after Taiwan has fallen. They will not suspect that we would make such a bold move so quickly and surprise will play a big part in the success of the entire operation."

Jet nodded understanding and added, "Comrade, remember the old Chinese proverb? 'In every crisis lies the seed of opportunity.'"

President Hu smiled at his old friend and replied, "Yes, I remember; haven't we lived our lives on the tail of that dragon?"

Then continuing added, "I will be sending you the action plan within thirty days or so. I want you to go through it with a fine-tooth comb and be certain that we are not overlooking any opportunity. This will be a lightning strike that the world will not see coming and we have to secure power within the first 48 hours or it could fail. Don't you agree?"

"Of course and if I might offer one piece of advice it would be that the shock troops must kill as many of the defenders as possible in the first hours. It needs to be a blood bath of gargantuan proportions with no quarter given to the enemy and the enemy is anyone with a weapon."

President Hu looked at his old friend and constant companion and shaking his head observed, "If you had been on the other side, we would still be licking the Americans boots. I never cease to be amazed. Thank you, old friend."

CHAPTER TWO

Good to his word, the action plan arrived by armed courier, with a six-man military escort, on the twenty-eight day after Jet and the Supreme leaders meeting.

The documents were hand written and there was a warning at the bottom of each page that should the documents be subjected to a temperature of over 32 Celsius (89.6 F.) or to any bright light the ink would disappear, which ruled out photocopying.

Jet's mind, always looking for an advantage or an edge, in any situation, immediately laid out the cover page on his desk, took out his I-phone and clicked a picture. The picture showed his desk top, with a clear white piece of paper in the middle of the frame. The same results were obtained when he used his I-pad and his electronic camera.

The sly fox smiled to himself and heard himself say, 'Well Comrade, now I am the one that is glad you are on our side.'

Setting down in an elegant side chair from the Jin Dynasty (265-420AD), his glasses perched on the edge of his nose, he briefly looked across the ornately landscaped garden, to the deep blue sea beyond. His mind settled into a cool and calculated state of being that he had always been able to control and he devoured the pages in less than an hour. Sipping his drink of choice, that staff kept at the ready 24/7, (Hokusetsu diaginjo YK35 shizukuzake titanium gold's sake), he stared at the whitecaps dancing over the ocean and tried to find a flaw in what he had just read. His mind recalled each and every major milestone and the continuity was there, the planning and preparation were clearly set forth and a smile lite up his face as he realized that he was looking at the future of the world and the future was total Chinese domination.

THE ARMY WITHIN ZHANLUE

Letting his mind drift he could envision the day when only orientals of Chinese ancestor inhabited the world. There would be no race problems, no communication problems and the planet would race through the universe as the Gods had always intended. CHINESE....

As Jet read the action plan, he had made cryptic notes in a small silk covered note book. Notes that no one but he could decipher and picking up the book he wondered out to the edge of the patio and inhaled a chest full of pure salt tainted air and congratulated himself on being one of the luckiest people to have ever ridden the blue planet.

Standing on the edge of the world, he ran down the notes; item by item and the zhanlue, while complicated, was in reality very simple and straight forward, for his incredible mind to grasp and comprehend. He smiled to himself, as the gentle breezes flowed past, and reminded himself that, 'Of course, but then the Supreme leader says I'm a genius so it shouldn't be difficult to understand a plan, most of which was from my original input.'

Stepping back in time he recalled formulating the plan during the early days of the Trump administration.

First, take advantage of America's broken borders.

Second, take advantage of the open society where people are free to move about without central government approval or knowledge.

Three, use the money they give you for goods and services to finance the operation.

Four, use TikTok and other social media and well as the general liberal media to influence the population and to spread propaganda.

Five, be bold. Take decisive action from the very first minute and spill as much blood as required be it military, local police and government officials, professors, students or anyone that shows any level of resistance.

Six, secure the food supply chain and use it as your ultimate weapon against the population.

Seven and lastly give the enemy no quarter, whatsoever. Follow instructions or meet your maker is the creed that each of our soldiers will follow.

Jet reviewed the overall zhanlue for the last time, convinced that it would be difficult, many of his countrymen and the invading army would die, but the goal of world domination requires total sacrifice and his country had the population to take a twenty-five or maybe even a thrifty-five percent loss and still outnumber the enemy.

Returning to his chair, he picked up his I-phone off a meter square solid block of green jade that served as a side table and texted a message to his leader's private phone.

> *"Review completed. No suggested changes. When you establish firm time frame please advise. Documents destroyed this date"* (signed simply – JHC.)

On the side of the patio was a cook center, in stainless steel, that featured three built in wok stations and a large barbecue. Jet fired up one of the woks, placed the dispatch papers in the center and watched the smoke curl up and over the retaining wall that kept the mountain side from washing into the patio area when the torrential winter rains hit the small island.

CHAPTER THREE

D-day was projected to be July 4, 2026, exactly two hundred and fifty years into the American experiment. A mere drop in the bucket, Jet concluded, 'When you consider China will be celebrating the year of the Snake 4722."

The guts of the plan was simple, and there would be hot spots not anticipated but overall America would cease to exist as a military challenge and we shall use their vast food production lands and agricultural technology to feed those we allow to enjoy the blue planet ride.

About three quarters of the way down the opening page, of his silk cover notebook, was a lone number. Jet kept looking at the number and trying to put it into some kind of context but his mind couldn't seem to make a connection.

He had seen military parades of a hundred thousand men and it was always impressive but this number, 4 million was larger than the USA military (2.1 million), all the policeman and sheriff deputies and all the FBI agents combined.

Who were these people? Why would they do the Chinese bidding and what did they want, or for that matter what would they demand in the future. How would they be controlled? Would they follow orders and if so, what was the motivation that made them leave their homeland and their loved ones? Jet smiled his big Cheshire cat grin as he knew the answer, the age-old answer. GREED. Of course it was greed. Most of the foot soldiers had a minimum education, most were dirt poor and this was their one opportunity to give their families and loved ones all that America could provide; and if it meant killing the locals, so be it…

For the past five years Chinese embassy offices around the world had been soliciting 16- to 30-year-old males to join the movement, offering them money to emigrate to America, all expenses paid. The Chinese embassy in Mexico City had worked tireless with the Mexican cartels to help the selected emigrants cross the southern US border and the staff of over one-hundred and fifty military officers had been hard pressed to develop the systems to keep track of the almost four-million-foot soldiers that were already in American, draining millions of dollars out of the local, state and federal government coffers. Sanctuary states like California were offering free medical care and New York City was floating an idea to give each emigrant ten thousand dollars. The brain-dead politicians were able to justify giving illegals money while ignoring the homeless America citizen veterans. The Chinese leaders shook their heads in disbelief as the American politicians dug their hole deeper. Jet thinking about the developments of the past three years, smiled and thought to himself, 'the deeper they dig the hole the easier it will be to bury them.'

Another important number in Jet's silk covered diary was 3142. The number of counties in the 50 states. Each county was assigned to a mid to top ranked army officer and as he looked out over the beautiful blue ocean, from his estate's veranda, he knew that some of those officers had been in place for over two years.

These undercover officers were serving as janitors, cooks, farm workers and a thousand other occupations. Each was wearing an ear implanted computer chip that allowed the embassy in Mexico City to not only track them but to alert them to upcoming instructions and to gather reports.

Each county commander was given the responsibility to chart and map each military installation within his county as well as each police station, sheriff office, FBI office and any other federal and state government buildings or installations. This data helped the planning groups determine the manpower that each county would need to take over the governmental installations listed above. For example if the

National Guard installation in Barstow, California, located in the country's largest county, San Bernardino, had fifty full time civil service workers and twenty-five enlisted army personnel then the planning group would assign enough personnel to that location to neutralize all the staff and take over operation of the facility and all the military hardware that the base controlled, from tanks, trucks, weapons and ammunition.

If, on D-day the U.S. Army activated all national guard troops and told them to report to their duty station, when they arrived the station would be controlled by the China forces that would neutralize the reporting members as not many would report with anything but a sidearm.

Military bases, training venues, missile launching bases and all military facilities in each county would be attacked by the highly armed Chinese forces. The element of surprise and the catastrophic and wholesale slaughter of American troops would bring the Pentagon to its knees in short order and would render the military ineffectual within hours.

All coastal naval installations would be invaded by ships of the Chinese Navy, to support the ground troops and only the U.S. Navy ships that were at sea would remain as a fighting force and each of them, wherever located in the world, would be targeted by Chinese war ships. The Chinese Navy would have been tracking each U.S. fighting ship, regardless of its location in the world, and would neutralize as many as possible. Those escaping would have no home port to escape to and would eventually have to surrender.

A missile defense system, similar to the Iron Dome that Israel uses, had been set up along the entire coast line of China and on the Indian, Tibet and Russian boarders so that any rouge nuclear U.S. submarines could be intercepted if they launched missiles towards the Chinese mainland.

Jet was certain that some Chinese cities would be impacted by weapons launched from American nuclear submarines but that was an acceptable cost the regime was willing to take. If, however, the takeover of each US military base, went without any serious glitches, the American submarines and war ships at sea would not be receiving communications from their superiors and few submarine commanders would be willing to launch a nuclear missile without direct orders.

The Pentagon alone would be overrun by a force of over one-hundred thousand troops that would have been mobilized for the July 4 attack. The U.S. government secret, high security communication centers had already been infiltrated by a group of undercover civil service workers and on D-day they would render the primary communication centers useless, as well as the backup centers that were scattered throughout the country.

Jet smiled to himself and said out loud, 'Sheer numbers are in our favor which means in the long run we will win. Getting there may be difficult and cost thousands upon thousands of lives, but not impossible.'

Sipping his drink of choice and taking in the ever-changing veranda view, Jet was reminded of one question that President Hu had asked, that had surprised the leader when Jet answered immediately, with a most unconventional view. The question was, 'Where would you base our American operation?' The immediate answer was, 'San Francisco.'

President Hu had given Jet a scrutinizing look, that made the moment one to remember and repeated, "San Francisco. I cannot believe you are serious."

Jet had replied, "Chinatown in San Francisco covers an area of thirty square blocks and is expanding daily and the population of seventy thousand has increased in the last year to just over one-hundred thousand and while some have ties to Taiwan most are loyal to your regime and at least ten thousand of the new arrivals are undercover agents that will lead the zhanlue."

THE ARMY WITHIN ZHANLUE

Jet recalled that President Hu had smiled at him and agreed that he could not argue with the logic or details of the zhanlue.

Jet's slip back into time was interrupted by his sister in laws announcement that dinner would be served in thirty minutes.

CHAPTER FOUR

Major Ka Kee Leung stepped off the Japan Airlines flight from Seoul to Mexico City airport, after a sixteen-hour flight and was greeted, after clearing customs, by a young man in civilian clothes, but who reeked of military bearing.

"Good morning, Sir, I am your contact and escort for the rest of the day. My name is Dan Lee."

"Well Mr. Lee it is nice to see a smiling face. What's our schedule look like?"

"Sir, we fly from here to Tijuana and then cross the border near San Diego and I should have you in San Francisco by early evening."

With a twinkle in his eye the Four-Star First-Class Colonel General, masquerading as a Major replied, "I look forward to watching the fog roll in over the Golden Gate Mr. Lee."

Good to his word, from his window seat at San Francisco's Cliff House restaurant, the General sipped a dry martini and watched the evening fog layer roll silently across the bay obscuring Alcatraz and the back reaches of the greatest bay on earth.

The General had released his escort upon arrival at SFO and had taxied to his second favorite restaurant in the City by the Bay. He was saving Scomas at Fisherman's Wharf for a special occasion, which would be coming up in a few days.

The General sat smugly watching the bay disappear and wondered if it was a sign from the God's. It could be he thought, just like America will disappear from the planet under the foggy cloud of Chinese brand communism.

The General almost laughed out loud when he thought of Biden trading, he and his son becoming millionaires, for America. It was laughable, but chilling as well to think that there were such people. It was a sober reminder to watch his back. After all, being the third highest ranking military officer in China was an awesome responsibility and you could never relax your grip, or as his tennis coach often said, "Relax your grip and you will find yourself facing an opponent with no racket."

Smiling to himself, after his third martini, the General remembered his humble beginnings, as the son of a rice grower, who escaped the farm to join the military and had the good fortune to serve under Jet How Chueng, who saw to it the young zealot moved up the ranks. He owed his position and his life to Jet and he had carried out Jet's orders with pride and efficiency, regardless of the carnage that his command rained down on the humble masses. Jet always said, "Our people are our strength and their blood greases the wheels of progress."

The taxi ride to the Holiday Inn Chinatown was uneventful as was the check in. The Presidential suite awaited the General and it was the very suite that Jet How had occupied so many years ago when he was working his Rainbow Zhanlue. "No calls until after ten," were the stern instructions that got the night clerks complete attention.

CHAPTER FIVE

United flight 95 departed SFO at 4:15 am and arrived in Chicago at 11.15 local time and Ka Kee was well rested having enjoyed the amenities of the first-class section on the Boeing 747.

The Chinese embassy driver was waiting for his important guest at the baggage claim area and in no time the embassies black limo was speeding down I-57 for Manteno. The fifty-mile drive took less than an hour and a few minutes after one pm the limo pulled into the Holiday Inn and Lin Wong was standing there with a handful of his underlings to welcome the third ranking officer in the Chinese Army.

"Good afternoon, Sir", Lin said as he opened the car door and greeted the smiling face of Ka Kee Leung for the very first time. Ka Kee looked at his host and thought, 'So this is their choice to lead the greatest takeover zhanlue the world will ever see. Interesting to say the least.' A shiver went up his spine and the words, 'watch your back' echoed and echoed across his brain.

Lin Wong was exceptional for a Chinese. He looked more like an Ohio State linebacker squinting at you from behind a massive face mask. His broad shoulders gave the illusion that his coat seams could snap at any moment and his Chinese/Mongolian features were handsome, as if chiseled out of jade.

"I hope you had a nice flight from San Francisco and that we can make your stay here informative and productive," Lin Wong said with a hint of apprehension in his voice.

"Thank you. Thank you very much."

The two men strolled thru the Holiday Inn lobby to the elevator and just the two of them made the ride to the fourth-floor suite that served as Lin Wong's home base.

"I have arranged a lite lunch for just the two of us and then later I would like to show you the plant site."

Ka Kee nodded approval and the two men removed their jackets and set down across from each other at a dining table that had a selection of small sandwiches and soft drinks arranged as upscale as the Holiday Inn in Manteno, Illinois could arrange.

"How long have you been here Lin?"

"Just starting my third month and to tell you the truth it seems more like three years. Things move so slow, so many restrictions and regulations and palms to grease. It certainly isn't like home and it is very frustrating to say the least."

"Ka Kee looked at the young man and with a big smile said, "Patience surly is a virtue."

Lin, smiled at his superior and his mind raced ahead and he thought, 'And old man when I am in charge of America and I am number two in the party, you shall still just be a General, so watch how you treat me.'

It was not a good start for either man and somehow the knew that the banging of heads would only lead to big headaches and they both decided, independently, but collectively to give each other space.

"Would it be possible to go to the construction site yet today?" Ka Kee asked.

"Of course, whenever you wish. It's not much more than a hole in the ground but we do have a scale model that will give you an idea as to what the completed project will look like."

The drive to the plant site, just south of town took only a few minutes and what had been a thousand-acre corn farm, since the late 1800's, was now a cyclone fenced area full of construction workers that were busy building forms and laying out the foundation of the new battery plant.

In his private construction trailer Lin showed Ka Kee the scale layout of the finished plant and it was a massive structure that would be capable of providing state of the art EV batteries and would employ over 2600 workers.

Looking at Ka Kee, Lin casually explained, "The State of Illinois gave us $536 million in tax credits and when we are finished the plant will employ over 2600 workers and all the raw materials will be imported from our homeland or other countries where we control the production. It is a sweetheart deal as the Americans would say."

Ka Kee nodded and in a low voice that only Lin could hear said, "For your information only the Biden family received over $5 million for helping this all come together."

Lin's eyes opened wide and he said, "Really?"

"Yes, really."

The evening meal at a local Chinese restaurant was not the Chinese gourmet fare that either man was use too but it was passable and they both laughed about how things would change in the years to come.

As they were riding the elevator up to the fourth-floor suite Lin asked, "What are your plans for tomorrow, Sir?"

"I plan to meet with our undercover agent who is in charge of this county. He served under me for years and I want to see the detailed plan he has worked up for this county." Smiling at his host he added, "It is interesting that we are in Kankakee county Illinois and my given name is the same as the last five letters."

Lin cocked his head and replied, "That has to be an omen of some kind Sir."

"Yes, that's the conclusion I came to when I first noticed the similarity. At any rate I will need a vehicle of some kind as I have arranged to meet my contact in a small town just down the 57 freeway a few miles."

Lin stood up and extracted a key from his inside coat pocket and said, "There is a red Toyota coupe in the parking lot that you are welcome to use."

Taking the key, the four-star first-class colonel general smiled at Lin and said, "Thank you. I'll try to get it back in one piece."

At seven the next morning Ka Kee was heading south and soon arrived at a little Marathon gas station, and good to his word the county captain was waiting for him. The Chinese man, dressed like an Illinois farmer, jumped into the passenger seat and the red Toyota made its way to a nearby public park.

The two men exited the car and meandered over to a picnic bench and Ka Kee said, "It is so nice to see you again comrade, what has it been two years?"

Yes, the middle-aged man nodded and added, "It's so nice to see you again Sir, as well."

"How is your life here Woo?"

"Well I am Frank to the locals and it is really better than I never could have imagined. I have become a part of the community and no one looks down on me or gives me any trouble because I am Chinese. I'm really just one of the guys and I enjoy the comradeship." With a deep frown on his face he added in a melancholic way, "It is going to be very difficult to pull the plug on these people when the time comes but I will do my duty. I will do my duty Sir."

Ka Kee looked at his old friend and nodded his understanding. "Frank, tell me about the structure in the county."

"Well Sir there is a County Administrator, a Finance Department, Highway Department, Planning Department, Maintenance Department along with the police and sheriff offices. All together there are about 60 law officers in the county. There are no military installations, other than two small National Guard units. I am putting together a unit of about 100 men that will take charge of the government functions on D-day. The core of the group will be twenty military comrades and the balance will be from the illegals that have come into the country over the past four years." Smiling he added, "They are all willing to lay their lives on the line for the piece of the pie I have promised them."

"Give me some examples of the pie."

"Yes, well they each will end up with hundreds of acres of good agriculture land, their pick of houses, their pick of wife's and their pick of businesses that might interest them."

"Their pick of wives?"

"Yes, as you know, most are single and have been living the single life and are just waiting for D-day so they can select the woman of their choice."

"Frank, is this going to work?"

"Sir, I have been thinking hard about that and I am certain that once we eliminate the authority's the rest of the population will fall into line. There will be lots of killing as we need to eliminate the current generation of the male leaders as well as their children. Most of the remaining population can be controlled by the allotment of food and by the strong hand of our men."

"Frank, I know this is being hard for you but think of the future. We will be riding a planet for the rest of time that is only Chinese. There will be no races to deal with as the non-Chinese in our ranks will be weeded out as soon as we have cemented power and control of this particular piece of real estate. Just Chinese citizens that appreciate what their leaders have envisioned for them and their off springs. It will be utopia, Frank, so instill resolve in your men and all will go as planned. You are the heart and soul of the movement and don't forget it."

"Thank you, Sir. It is difficult sometimes to see the big picture. Would you like the details on the Kankaee targets that we will eliminate on D-day?"

The Colonel nodded yes, and Frank rolled out his well-worn map, on the park picnic table, and started his rehearsed chronicle.

"On D-day we shall have an armed, uniformed force of just over three hundred commandos to neutralize all country and city government locations including the two National Guard installations.

That will include all sheriff, police and fire station locations. We will eliminate the morning shift and will send out our troops, in the government patrol vehicles, and if they encounter any hostility, from the general population or from off-duty officers, we will eliminate those threats as well."

Frank paused and waited for his superior to react to the plan.

"Frank, if all the other 3142 county commanders are as prepared as you are, the takeover of America will be measured in mere days. You have done an exceptional job of research and organization."

With a sheepish grin, Frank looked at his superior and thanked the Gods that he had been born Chinese and then asked, "Can you tell me exactly how we will be provided with uniforms and arms?"

"Of course; between the end of this year and D-Day you will receive a container that will contain about 290 boxes, each consigned to a specific man. You will put the boxes in a commercial storage facility and distribute them to your men about ten days before D-day. If your county requires more than that number a second, third or fourth container will be shipped to you. Each box will contain uniforms, firearms and identification tags. Since we have each commando's life details and each has an ear implant, we will have no trouble providing these items in the proper sizes. The identification tags will only be activated when they are passed near the commando's implant. If the identification tags are not activated by the ear implant, then none of the firearms provided will be operational. In other words none of the firearms will be operational unless the proper ear implant activates the identification tags. This will preclude the shipment having any value to anyone other than the addressee."

Frank nodded understanding and continued by asking, "Is it possible for you to give me the details on the how the chip project works? I have heard bits and pieces but don't really understand the overall program, but maybe I don't need to know."

"Well it is an interesting part of warfare that has never been tried on a large scale. We used it first when we wiped out ISIS but that's another story. At any rate I will give you just the basics." The First-Class Colonel General looked across the table and decided that just the short version was necessary. No need to burden Frank with all the details that had been part of Jet How Cheung's master plan for the past ten years. The Colonel General smiled to himself and remembered the flashing eyes and excitement level that Jet seldom allowed to be seen when he explained the program to the Colonel and the other hand-full of top-ranking military officers that were assembled in the President's underground bunker.

Jet had started the presentation by stating, unequivocally that in the next ten years the computer chip industry would be the very backbone of the military industrial complex. The Colonel remembered Jet's exact words, "If we control the computer chip industry, we will control the world."

Jet had gone on to explain that all of the other world powers would be leery if Chinese chips ended up in their war machines, but that the world would flock to buy and use chips coming from a neutral alley like Taiwan. So the challenge was to infiltrate the Taiwan Chip industry and add a dead-end switch to each chip that could be activated by special electronic signals. "We did that", Jet told his audience, "By blackmailing high ranking Taiwan military officers who had parents on the mainland like General-Half-Ear and his longtime associate Frank Fan."

Colonel General Ka Kee looked at his friend and said, "Taiwan has not shipped a chip to the west, for the past ten years, that we cannot disable, which means we can shut down the American trucking industry, the airline industry, and the communication industries as well as most electrical generating plants, manufacturing plants and last but not least the great, invincible American military machine will be on foot. Did I answer your question?"

Frank was big eyed. The answer was more than he could digest and all he could do was nod his head to the question.

Swallowing deep he ask in a shaky voice, "Will you be staying here for awhile.?"

"No, Ill drive back to the Holiday Inn and then fly out of Chicago tomorrow morning. I have several other county commanders I want to see." Adding with a big smile, "I hope they are as well prepared as you, my old friend." Cocking his head and looking directly into Franks eyes, the Colonel asked, "What are your plans after D-day is over and the mission accomplished?"

Frank, starring out into the surrounding corn fields replied, "I would just like to spend some quite time with my wife and children on a local farm that has its own lake and creek. It is nearby if you would like to see it."

"No, not today but I promise to come visit you after this is all over. It would be a special treat that I look forward to, so stay well old friend," and then after a short pause added; "You don't have to be on the frontline you know, that's what the young commandos are for."

Frank smiled and replied to quiety, "Thank you, thank you very much for allowing me a small part in such a grand plan."

On the drive back to the Holiday Inn Ka Kee watched the landscape slip by and was taken with the beauty of the countryside and could not help noticing the contrast between Illinois and his Chinese homeland. At home the road would have been crowed with people hurrying here and there, on every kind of conveyance known to man and with unbelievable loads of this and that. Just too many people for the land he thought. He made himself a promise that he would do all in his power to not let that happen in America and for that matter the rest of the world that China would acquire once America was gone. The word 'GENOCIDE' passed in and out of his brain and he knew that millions on the blue planet would die before the utopia that his superiors envisioned became a reality.

CHAPTER SIX

Ka Kee settled deep in his first-class seat, closed his eyes and reviewed his meeting with Frank Woo as United Airlines flight 76 made its way south toward downtown Louisville, Kentucky.

Kankakee county, Illinois was a cakewalk compared to the hundreds of metropolitan areas that dotted the American landscape and he knew that the challenges in the major population centers would be extremely complicated.

Not only were their major military bases to deal with but the infrastructure of hospitals, universities, and large federal and state governmental agencies, all which needed to be neutralized.

The hospitals in America, all 6120 of them, would be a major challenge. Commandos with medical backgrounds would be assigned to each venue and D-day would see the halting of admissions, except of course for any injured commandos. All ambulance vehicles would be chip disabled, emergency rooms would be closed and all current patients would be cleared out and sent home. This would result in thousands and thousands of deaths but it was a necessary part of the program. The hospital staffs would be given temporary furloughs except for a skeleton crew that would keep the facilities open and operational so that when the takeover was complete, they could be brought back on line.

Ka Kee smiled to himself as he brought another important segment of the American experience up from his fertile brain. The academic population was an often-overlooked segment of any society, yet they were the reservoir from which the anti-establishment protests were stuffed. In 2019 there had been over 370,000 Chinese nationals attending American universities. These were the children of the elite society that thrived in China and Jet How had used them to greatly influence the 2020 election. He had organized them into hate Trump squads and they helped turn the tide that saw Joseph Robinette Biden Jr. ascend the throne.

There were only around 290,000 students in country at the present, but over fifty percent of them had ear tags and were standing ready when their country called them to duty. They would be the backbone of the takeover and would fill the government jobs necessary to keep the country operating. In the long run they would have a big impact in the conversion of America from an English-speaking country to a Chinese speaking country.

'It was just too easy,' Ka Kee thought as he sipped the Napa Valley Champaign and watched the green country side slide under the wing.

The arrival in Louisville was uneventful and within an hour of touch down Ka Kee found himself setting at the bar in the Executive Inn, outside of town, enjoying another glass of the Napa Valley grape juice. He had stayed there before and enjoyed the total greenery of the surrounding countryside and it was just a short cab ride to town.

Over his shoulder Ka Kee heard, "Mr. Leung I presume?" Ka Kee turned around on the swivel bar stool to find a smiling Chinese face, with a receding hair line and an oval face that accented the slant eyes which were covered by the bushiest eyebrows he had ever seen on an oriental. "Yes, I'm Ka Kee Leung and I assume you are P.K. Fong?"

"Yes, I am and it is so nice to finally meet you." Pausing the eyes twinkled under the bushy eye brows P.K. asked, "Would you like to go to the restaurant or would you prefer a table here in the bar?"

"Neither" Ka Kee replied, "I think it would be better to confine our conversations to the walls of my room, follow me."

The Executive Inn was a standard three-story motel/hotel combination that reminded you of any Roadway or Best Western scattered across the country. P.K. followed Ka Kee out of the bar, down a long hallway and to a ground floor room that opened onto a courtyard that featured a pool at the far end. It was a suite, so the living room offered a large couch and several comfortable easy chairs.

Ka Kee removed his coat, plopped down in one of the chairs and indicated P.K. should occupy the couch.

"Where did you grow up?" Ka Kee asked.

"Shanghai, so I am a city boy. My father was a caretaker at the Yu Garden complex, if your familiar with that landmark."

"Yes, I have. It's a marvels venue and I remember the grounds were immaculate, thanks to your father, I'm sure."

P.K. nodded and continued, "I excelled in school and was selected to be sent to an American university and luckily, I ended up at the University of Louisville. Have been here for six years and during the 2020 elections, I lead the pro-Biden group on campus."

"I assume that you have an ear implant?"

"Yes Sir, that's correct and as you know I am the Jefferson county commander. Since 2003, Louisville's borders have been the same as those of Jefferson county and that takes in a population of almost eight hundred thousand. There are about four hundred sheriff officers and just over a thousand police officers so I am assembling a team of almost two thousand commandos that will eliminate those departments on D-day. In addition I have another two thousand men that will take over all the government offices, hospitals and of course all the higher education facilities."

P.K. paused and asked, "Would you like to see my maps that pinpoint our initial attack points?"

"No, that's not necessary, but I would like you to tell me about your chain of command."

"Of course. There are over twenty-line officers from the People's Liberation Army that are drawing up all the details for D-day. We will have every government venue covered and will neutralize as many of the enemy as possible in the first hours. As you know Fort Knox is just thirty miles southwest and we have been coordinating with the commanders in Bullit, Hardin and Mead counties as Fort Knox is in all three counties. If they need our assistance in neutralizing Fort Knox and the depository, we shall be ready to send them additional troops."

Ka Kee smiled at his bushy eyed subordinate and said, "For your information only, as soon as Americas air defense system is neutralized, we will send all sixty-seven of our Y-20 air cargo carriers to the Louisville airport and we will load each with their maximum payload of 73 tons and will fly the contents of the Fort Knox depository, to the homeland. That means that within a few days after D-day every ounce of Americas 4581 tons of gold reserve will be in China."

For the first time in his life, P.K. was speechless. He just looked at his leader and thought how lucky he was to be a part of this grand operation. His dream of a Kentucky horse farm was actually on the horizon provided he didn't 'buy the farm' on or around D-day. Be careful and prudent and don't take any unnecessary chances. Let the shock troops do the dirty work, after all you are the leader and you are needed to lead up to D-day and beyond.

P.K. heard his name, and coming back to reality gushed his apologizes for his lapse. "Guess my brain just can't handle the magnitude of this operation, sorry sir."

Ka Kee smiled and asked, "Is there anything you need to bring your part of this operation to a successful conclusion?"

"No Sir, we have the bank funds necessary, we have thousands of our people in place; each has a specific job and I know that they are all as committed as I am so there is no doubt we will be successfully. I was wondering about uniforms and weapons and how that distribution will be made and when?"

Ka Kee gave P.K. the same speech he had given Frank Woo the day before and wondered how the warehouse operation was proceeding. Maybe next week he could fit a quick trip into Mexico to see how the operation was shaping up.

"Do you have any other questions?"

"Will I see you again before D-day?"

"I don't think so. I have a lot of ground to cover between now and then, but should you have any kind of problem, that seems insuperable just call me on this number."

Ka Kee handed P.K. a business card that had nothing but a telephone number. "Add a two to each number and you will reach my cell phone. Please only call in an emergency."

His flashing eyes made contact with the bushy eyes and P.K. knew that it would take a really serious problem for him to ever use the number.

Later in the day, after Ka Kee had reviewed all of P.K.'s maps, charts and manpower requirements he went out front to the waiting line of taxis and slipping into the back seat asking the driver, "Can you give me a tour of Fort Knox?"

"Of course Sir. Do you want to see inside the depository or just drive the grounds?"

"Just driving the grounds will be fine."

Three hours later the taxi dropped his fare in front of the New Orleans House in downtown Louisville, collected his two-hundred-dollar fare and a nice hundred-dollar tip.

Ka Kee made his way into the old brick five story building and was pleased to see P.K. waiting for him as previously arranged.

"I was here several years ago and vowed if I was ever within a hundred miles of Louisville I would come here for the world's best seafood buffet."

"Yes, it is unusual Sir," P.K. replied.

Several hours later, as full as he could ever remember Ka Kee taxied back to the Executive Inn and was satisfied that the Jefferson County commander would do a good job of taking over Louisville and the surrounding areas.

He was pleased that P.K. had such a strong relationship with the Chinese Clubs at each of the eight four-year private colleges and universities in the area and that the student commandos would number almost two thousand individuals. The students would take over the reigns of the local governments and would be the backbone of the overall zhanlue. P.K. would of course direct the takeover and would operate out of the mayor's office with his group of Chinese Army officers.

Smiling, Ka Kee thought, 'Its going to difficult, we will loose a lot of people but in the end we will enjoy victory and I want to be here when the first Y-20 takes off for China with just over 70 tons of American gold.'

CHAPTER SEVEN

Since Louisville Ka Kee had logged St Louis, Omaha, Denver, Portland and Seattle and was currently flying into San Francisco for a few days' rest. His headquarters was the penthouse at the Chinatown Holiday Inn on Grant street and he loved being back in the city by the bay.

The afternoon fog was moving in as his United flight landed at SFO. The approach over the back bay waters was beautiful with the endless string of salt ponds that ranged in colors from burnt orange and red to glistening white. 'I think I will live here when this is all over,' Ka Kee caught himself thinking and smiled wondering if he would be one of the survivors or one of the causalities. The streets would run red before this zhanlue was over. It might take several years to pacify the surviving population but in the long run the zhanlue would work and the blue planet would go flying through future space with the oriental race in full charge.

Ka Kee was tired but the ride from SFO to the Holiday Inn went quickly and in no time, he found himself with his San Francisco staff enjoying a meal at his favorite Fisherman's Wharf restaurant, Scomas.

What a treat; dungeness crab, sour dough bread and wine from across the bay. The restaurant is tucked back in the back reaches of the wharf and most of the tourists never know what they are missing. Ka Kee and his staff had a memorable dinner and it was good to spend a night in familiar surroundings after his whirlwind trip across America. He vowed to take a few days off, maybe a drive up to Napa, over the Golden Gate bridge and some lunches to remember at the hundreds of wineries and restaurants that dot the countryside.

The envisioned hiatus from work was short lived and two days later he found himself on a flight from SFO to San Diego.

THE ARMY WITHIN ZHANLUE

Flying into San Diego reminded him of the old Hong Kong airport where you could look into the apartments as the plane threaded its way between the skyscrapers.

Dan Lee was johnny on the spot again and whisked Ka Kee out of the airport, into a waiting car and the driver headed south on Cal. 94 which dead-ends at the town of Tecata, Mexico.

Tecata is a sleepy little city just over the Mexican/American border and the mayor and his staff were standing in front of the Restaurante Amores when Ka Kee and Dan Lee arrived.

Dan and the mayor seemed like old friends and introductions went quickly. The mayor was a portly man with a big mustache and a bigger smile. As he shook hands with the honored guest, he was calculating the millions that this man was bringing to the table. 'Praise the saints,' he thought to himself as his mind raced ahead and he could see the villa on the Gulf of California that would proclamation to the world that Mayor Ruiz was one of the biggest personalities in all of Mexico.

In a private dining room, the party of eight were treated to a real Mexican fiesta lunch and the host was quick to point out to his honored guest the dishes that were really hot, with a splash of belly laughter.

In the back of the room was a large table with a scale model of the project and after lunch the mayor explained to his guest the details of the operation. The building was in the center of a 100 acre stretch of desert, just two miles south of the Mexican border and three miles to the east of Tecata. The entire property was surrounded by a cyclone fence on the outside parameter that was twenty foot tall and extended into the sandy soil another twenty feet and metal detecting sensors were positioned every Twelve inches to a depth of ten feet. The top of the fence had three layers of QVQE razor wire. One layer on top inside, one on top outside and one in the center. The inside fence was fifteen feet from the outside fence and was an exact duplicate. The building was a tilt-up concrete structure that was forty feet high, by 800 feet long by 400 feet wide making it the largest building in

Mexico. The land had been given to a Mexican company by the government of Tecata and the Baja California state government and carried tax free status for fifteen years. The Mexican company was the same company that had offices in Mexico City, where the tracking of emigrants to America was overseen by one-hundred and fifty Chinese Army personnel.

"When will the building be operational," Ka Kee asked the Mayor, and hedging just a bit the Mayor replied, "By the end of this month Senior, if all goes as planned," and then as an afterthought, continued, "We are having some trouble tying the access road into the 94 freeway, but that should be resolved shortly." Continuing he added, "The gringos are dragging their heels on the new boarder control station, but we have greased enough palms that it too will be operational by month end, or by the middle of next month at the very latest."

The big smile from under the mustache gave Ka Kee a strange feeling, but time really was not that critical so he let it pass.

"Mayor, please let me know when we can start shipping merchandise out of the warehouse and across the border. We want to get that up and running as soon as possible."

"Of course senior, I will keep in constant contact with Dan Lee and I'm sure he will keep you appraised."

Dan nodded in the affirmative and Ka Kee was taken back when the mayor asked, "What kind of merchandise will you be shipping out of the center?" The minute it was out, the mayor knew he had stepped in the horse manure but Ka Kee simply replied, "Just general household items and clothing, like any big department store might sell."

Continuing, Ka Kee asked, "Have you been receiving your payments on time?"

"Oh, si senior, very timely, very nice, thank you so much." Then continuing he added, "We have noticed all the interior workers are Chinese, will there be a time when you can employ our local labor? They will work very hard for you I know."

"Yes, as the operation is refined we will transfer the Chinese workers and will, of course, replace them with your hard working citizens, Mr. Mayor, you can count on it."

The ride back to the San Diego airport was quick and half way there, Dan Lee asked, "Comrade, can you tell me the real purpose of the warehouse or is that classified?"

Ka Kee leaned back in the plush seat of the limo closed his eyes and said, "You are an escort and courier and if you need to know such information, I am sure your superiors would have told you. What is your rank?"

"Captain sir."

"Well, when you get back to your base, report to your commanding officer and tell him I have requested that you be demoted to Lieutenant and sent back to China immediately. Am I understood Lieutenant?"

Dan Lee saw his career and his life vanish and he dammed all his ancestors for creating such a stupid person.

The limo pulled up to the curb, in front of United Airlines and Ka Kee exited the vehicle without a further word.

Dan Lee had the limo drop him at Delta Airlines, just down the concourse, walked inside, bought a ticket on the next flight to Cancun, Mexico and was never heard from again.

CHAPTER EIGHT

One star General, Lin Lau was in a relative good mode which percolated down the ranks of the Mexican warehouse staff, which numbered over three hundred, all of which were Chinese Army personnel.

In one corner of the huge warehouse, sleeping and latrine facility had been set up, and it was a twelve hour on, twelve hour off work day, seven days a week for the entire staff. No trips to Tecata or anywhere else to break the routine.

It had just been twenty-eight days since the last construction worker departed and the building was operational with power supplied by a bank of generators and water from a well that was over fifteen hundred feet deep. A natural gas line that ran along the border had been tapped so the operation was completely self-sufficient and product had been arriving at the rate of fifteen to twenty, forty-foot containers, every day.

The supply chain was unique in that all the containers coming in from China were off loaded at the port of Long Beach and trucked to the warehouse in Tecata via Interstate 5 and California 94. It was only a 123-mile run and China had obtained permission from the United States State Department to forgo any duties and inspection, in that all the merchandise was destined for Mexico, and would not have any economic impact on the American economy.

At the back side of the warehouse, in the southeast corner, a complete clothing manufacturing plant was taking shape as well as an assembly plant for the manufacturing of a new plastic based assault rifle and a plastic base 9mm hand gun. The rifle and pistol parts had been printed on a 3-D printer so the operation in Tecata was strictly an assembly function. Each of the guns used a standard 9mm round and were only capable of firing ten clips of fifteen rounds each before reaching the point where the barrel needed to be replaced. Each firearm also contained a computer chip that had to be activated by the users ear tag and the universal identification tags before it became operational.

The firearms would be useless without bullets so each operator in America would be instructed to purchase 500 rounds of standard 9mm ammunition before D-day.

General Lin Lau was tall for a Chinese, almost 6'3" and had a presence that intimidated most everyone he met. His staff was gun shy in that he blamed them for every little delay or problem and the blame was not couched in niceties. He had been aware that Ka Kee was in Tecata and was upset that his superior had not seen fit to tour the facility, but Mayor Ruiz had called him and said that Ka Kee was running late and that he had apologized for missing the scheduled tour.

Lin Lau had a golf cart, as did his five underlings, that oversaw the day to day operations, and he raced around the complex keeping tabs on every phase of the project.

Now that the machinery was installed, the actual manufacturing process was underway and Chinese Army uniforms were starting to come off the line. The production staff had the measurements of all the operators in America and there were only four different size uniforms that had to be manufactured so it was not a complicated process. Before the uniforms could be boxed, however, each needed the shoulder patches that identified each particular unit and the proper rank designations.

In the main warehouse area, row after row of pallet racks were being installed. Each rack was five pallets high, and each rack was designated with code numbers that identified the state and county location. Each state had a designated area as did each county and the two million uniforms, consigned to each location, would have to be boxed and ready for shipment by the last day of May 2025. The identification tags had already been produced by a factory in China and they only needed to be matched with the uniform and the firearm assigned to each individual.

Lin Lau, reviewing the time tables with his staff was pleased to see that the projections showed that the 2 million boxes would be completed by the end of January 2026, so if all went as planned he could shut down the operation and join his unit in North Carolina well before D-day. Starting next month he would need to ship ten containers per day to meet the January 2026 deadline. Each 40-foot container would contain 290 boxes and each would be consigned to a county commander who would rent commercial storage spaces to store the units. By the end of January 2026 over 6000 containers would have been shipped and the two million boxes would be in each county waiting for distribution a few days before D-day.

The meeting over and day almost finished, the General opened his private I-pad and typed a short message, in Chinese to Ka Kee.

"Sir, on schedule to ship ten containers, each with 290 boxes, per day to north American locations starting in less than 30 days. Hope you will be able to schedule visit to our operation. Please provide special import documentation so containers will not have to be inspected at USA border." Lin Lau

Lin starred at the communication and wondered out loud, "I wonder how many Gringos got their palms greased to pull off 6000 containers, from Mexico to USA without inspection or duty?"

Little did he know that the greasy Gringo was named Hunter.

CHAPTER NINE

On the flight back from San Diego to San Francisco Ka Kee leaned back in his first-class seat, sipping a nice Chardonay from Napa and smiled as he thought of his new Mexican friend Mayor Ruiz. With the amount of money the Mayor was collecting, under the table from China, he should end up a very rich man and Ka Kee wondered if he might be a safety valve of some kind if the Zhanlue was not successful.

He came out of his day-dream, bolted straight up in the seat and asked himself, 'Could that be possible?' Relaxing a little he reviewed the possibilities. 'Of course, it could all go south in a hundred ways. A slip of the tongue here, a defection, or a million different ways, Yes, it could go south, but the likely hood of that happening was not likely.'

'Don't go there again', he warned himself and looked out the window at the vast Pacific ocean and the clouds blowing in form Asia. Smiling he reminded himself, 'The clouds blow in from Asia just like we will and America will be blanketed by an unstoppable force.'

The traffic wasn't too bad from SFO to his Chinatown hotel and after a quick shower and change of clothes he was ready to face the Committee of Eight.

The Committee had an office nearby on Kearny street and he opted to stretch his legs and make the hilly walk. The sign on the building announced that this was the home of "The Chinatown Committee of Eight".

Ka Kee entered and found himself in an elegant 18th Century hotel lobby complete with brass spittoons and overstuffed furniture from the period. A counter in the back of the room was manned by an extremely attractive woman that Ka Kee judged to be in her mid-thirties. Before he could say anything, she came from behind the counter to greet him and said, "Ka Kee Leung, I presume?"

"At your service miss."

"Won't you please follow me, the committee is assembled and has been awaiting your arrival."

Turning on her heels she crossed the room and led him down a hall to a large conference room where eight smiling faces were seated at a round conference table that had to be ten feet in diameter and was made from one piece of polished redwood.

Ka Kee enjoyed the walk as the hips in front of him swayed nicely and the red silk covering left little to the imagination.

The eight smiling faces, six men and two women all rose to greet the honored quest and an elderly gentlemen with a white go-tee said, "Comrade Leung we are pleased to make your acquaintance and we welcome you to our humble quarters. My name is Wuhan and I am the current chairman of our 'Gang of Eight', as we call ourselves. The name plates in front of each person are for your information. We cannot tell you how thrilled we are to have you join us this evening, and of course we are extremely excited about the prospects of working with you."

The silk hips lady, indicated that Ka Kee should be seated, next to the chairman, and then took a seat to the side and prepared to document the evenings proceedings with pad and pencil.

"Thank you, Chairman Wuhan," and nodding to the others continued, "I am here at the request of the President of China who is well aware of the work that your committee undertakes."

Eyes lite up around the table and glances of wonder were exchanged as Ka Kee continued, "The Chairman thinks that the expansion of Chinatown, here in San Francisco, is a good thing for Chinese/American relations and in fact he is encouraging the Chinatown areas, in every major American city to expand. To that end he wishes to help you increase your area from the current size of about thirty square blocks to double that size over the next few years."

Ka Kee paused to let the information just provided sink in and than added, "And to that end we propose to fund your organization with an initial grant of fifty million dollars for the acquisition of additional property, especially condominiums or apartment buildings."

Murmurs of excitement went up around the table and Chairman Wuhan asked, "Sir, can you tell us why we were selected?"

"Of course, your Chinatown is the largest concentration of Chinese people outside of Asia and the world is moving closer and closer to a centralized government and we want our fellow comrades to have as large a voice as possible when these changes come to pass. I know you all read the newspapers, so you know that over twenty-four thousand Chinese nationals have crossed the Mexican/American boarder in just the past twelve months; illegally, and since Biden took office the number may be double or triple."

Ka Kee paused and the continued in a low voice, "These are Chinese citizens, fellow countrymen and ancestors of us all; and they need jobs, places to live so they can raise families and expand our influence over this great land."

Turning to Chairman Wuhan, Ka Kee asked, "Will you help us take care of our brothers?"

The Chairman looked around the table, making eye contact with each member and then looking at Ka Kee with incredible empathy replied, "Yes, General we will help you."

"Good, the President will be pleased; I can assure you the President will be very pleased. In the near future I will introduce you to an associate that will have the ability to oversee the transfer of the funds and will also, with your permission, review the investments that you plan to make. He will be with you until the bulk of the money has been spent, with your approval, of course."

"Yes, yes that will be fine," Chairman Wuhan gushed and if you do not have any further business can we all go upstairs to our private dining room? We have prepared some very special dishes for you."

Ka Kee smiled and replied, "Only if the young lady can join us."

Chairman Wuhan looked at Ka Kee and said, "Of course my granddaughter would enjoy that I am sure."

CHAPTER TEN

Ka Kee's meeting with the Gang of Eight was just twelve days ago, but in that time he had been in six states and talked to over thirty county commanders. Each meeting went similar to the P.K. Fong meeting in Louisville and so far none, of the county commanders, had been a disappointment and he was glad to be back in San Francisco.

Bank of America, in San Francisco, is located in a fifty-two story, 779 feet skyscraper at 555 California Street and the International section occupies the twenty-ninth floor. Ka Kee was in the customer waiting room, promptly at 10am waiting for the courier from China to make his appearance.

A few minutes before ten, a small, balding Chinese man with a large briefcase entered the waiting room, and looking around and seeing Ka Kee rushing over to him asking, "Are you General Leung?"

"Yes, Comrade, and you must be Wo Hoing."

"Yes, Sir I am. This is only my second trip abroad and I have been worried that I would not be able to locate you. I am so relieved to find you, so relieved."

"Well, Mr. Hoing you can relax. After our meeting with the bank, I will take your hotel where I am sure you will be comfortable. Do you have luggage?"

"Yes, my suitcase is out in the hall."

"Well, bring it in and it will be safe while we visit with the bankers."

Wo rushed out and came back rolling a suitcase that was just about as big as he was.

Walking over to the receptionist Ka Kee asked, "May my associate leave his bag here while we are meeting with Mr. Armacost?"

"Of course Sir, and Mr. Armacost just advised that he will be with you momentarily."

Before he could say thank you, a door on the far side of the room opened and Chief of the International section asked, "Mr. Leung?"

"Yes, I am Ka Kee Leung and this is my associate from the Chinese government, Mr. Hoing."

"Won't you please come in? I have been looking forward to meeting you both."

The office was large and a modern stainless steel and glass desk was facing the corner window that had an unobstructed view of the Bay Bridge as it crossed Yerba Buena island on its way to Oakland.

A large conference table that seated twelve took up the remainder of the office space and Armacost indicated that Ka Kee and Wo should be seated.

"Well gentlemen, what can I do for you and the Chinese government?"

Ka Kee smiled at his host and replied, "We would like to negotiate a letter of credit from the Republic of China in the amount of 50 million dollars."

All Mike Aramacost could do was repeat the amount, "You did say 50 million U.S. dollars?"

"Yes, that is correct. May I have the documentation Wo?"

Wo stood up, put his briefcase on the table, punched in the combination, opened the flap and extracted a large manila envelope which he handed to Ka Kee.

Ka Kee opened the wax sealed envelope and removed a standard China Bank Letter of Credit certificate and slid it across the desk. "You will notice that the certificate has been signed and sealed by President Hu and before it is active both Mr. Hoing and I need to counter sign and add our thumb prints to the document. Will there be any delay in transferring the funds to a new account in Mr. Hoing's name?"

Mike Armacost picked up the certificate, walked over to the window, held it up to the light and recognized the certificates water marks, as he had seen thousands of Chinese credits, just never one of this size. Walking over to his desk, he punched the intercom and said, "Virginia, will you ask Brian to come to my office, immediately with the necessary forms for a new checking account and a finger print pad. Yes, immediately. Thank you."

With a twinkle in his eye, Mike eased into his chair and said, "I have to say General this is about the biggest deposit we have had in weeks." Then adding, "Mr. Hoing will this be in your name and will you be the only authorized signatory?"

Wo looked at the General for guidance and Ka Kee said, "The name on the account will be 'The Committee of Eight' and only Wo and I will have signatory rights."

Mike Armacost cocked his head and with a quizzical look said, "I have never heard of this committee. Is it a new organization here in the city?"

"No, it's not new. They have been active for the past ten years and their mission is to help Chinese people find homes and businesses in the Chinatown area or on it's fringes. You may not know, but San Francisco's Chinatown is the largest concentration of Chinese outside of Asia and we, the Chinese government, are just helping our brothers in America find a better life. It is part of the President Hu's humanitarian and ancestral efforts and is not confined to just America, but to many other countries as well."

"I had no idea. So the funds will be dispersed basically to purchase property?"

"That is correct, in fact", looking hard at Wo, "That is the only reason, so each check will probably be size-able. You may want to add that notation to your master files so we will not experience any undue delays."

"Of course. Will the checks required two signatures?"

"No."

A knock at the door, announced Brian's arrival with the proper forms, and within twenty minutes the matter was concluded.

"Will you be staying in San Francisco long.?

"Hoing will be here until the money is gone and I am here for several months. I'm headquartered at the Holiday Inn in Chinatown, penthouse, and if you are ever in the mood for an unusual Chinese lunch or dinner give me a call." Smiling Ka Kee added, "Don't think many of you gringos know the small out of the way Chinese venues."

"That would be a treat. I'll definitely take you up on your offer. Is there anything else we can do for you today?"

"No, I think that does it and I would like to thank you and your staff for an unusual banking experience." Mike walked his guests to the outer door and all the way he was calculating the daily interest on 50 million. His income flow chart would be at the top of the heap for the next few months. "Thank you, President Hu!" he mouthed.

Ka Kee lead Wo down to the ground floor, pulling his giant suitcase. The ride to the Holiday Inn, which was less than a mile away, would take thirty minutes, because of the traffic and all the one way streets, but it gave Ka Kee adequate time to impart a strict set of operational guidelines.

"Wo, when the account gets down to the hundred thousand dollar range, you have my permission to close the account and withdraw the remaining funds in cash."

Wo starred at the third ranking officer in the Chinese army and started to ask a question, but the sober look and the flashing eyes, that looked back at him, made the little mans lips go tight.

"You will take out five thousand as a bonus and the balance you will deposit in a Bank Of America safety deposit box. You will keep one key and you will mail the other to me at the Holiday Inn. Questions?"

"No, Sir I understand and I will follow your instructions to the letter."

"Tomorrow we will get you installed at the Committee of Eight headquarters and I want you to be certain that none of the funds are spent on anything but acquiring property, all which must be on the current fringe of Chinatown. You only answer to me and you make sure that the Committee does not use any of the funds for anything but property acquisition. Understood?"

"Yes, General, understood."

"After you are installed in the hotel, come up to the penthouse and we will go to dinner at my favorite restaurant at Fisherman's Wharf."

CHAPTER ELEVEN

Dinner at Scoma's was once again incredible as the maitre d', an ex-prize fighter with shoulders broader than Sylvester Stallone's, and Ka Kee had become fast friends over the past weeks. The excessive tips might have accounted for the friendship, but that was just Ka Kee's style.

The dungeness crab (Metacarcinus magister) arrived on boats that docked next to the restaurant, so freshness was a given, and when combined with the unique San Francisco sour dough bread and Napa Valleys finest Chardonnay, Kongsgaard, at $1475 per bottle, what could be finer?

Wo Hoing had never experience service and food at this level and on the way back to the hotel he asked, "Comrade is everything in America this wonderful?"

Ka Kee smiled his imitation of Jet How's Cheshire cat grin and patting his companions knee and said, "Yes Wo, it is a marvelous country and one day you and I may get to live here permanently, if my mentor's plans come to fruition."

Wo did not understand any of the implications, just conveyed to him, by the third ranking official of his country, but the glow of the Chardonnay, erased any concerns.

Half way back to the hotel Ka Kee tapped the taxi driver on the shoulder and asked, "Can you drop us at the Gold Spike and wait while we have a drink?"

The hundred dollar bill that remained on the drivers would ensured that the answer would be yes."

The taxi screeched to a stop at 527 Columbus Street, and Ka Kee almost drug Wo across the sidewalk and through the aging doors that desperately need a coat of paint. The space was only twenty feet wide and forty feet long with a bar down one side of the room.

The bartender, one Don Zavattero, who's family had start the bar in 1946, gave Ka Kee a big welcome smile and immediately reached under the bar and pulled out one of the six bottles in his stock of Kongsgaard Chardonnay."

Giving Ka Kee a big smile, Don said, "I invested half a years profit in stocking this stuff for you, glad you came back."

"Don't worry my man, you can count on me drinking it all."

An hour later, supporting Wo, Ka Kee made it out to the waiting taxi and said to the driver, "Head for the hotel my good man."

Wo did not get down to breakfast until Ka Kee had consumed his third cup of tea, and big-eyed explained, "Sorry I am late Sir, I might have had too much of that wine last night."

Ka Kee smiling said, "No problem. We have an appointment to get you installed at the Committee of Eight headquarters at eleven."

"I'll be ready, Sir. Should I met you in the lobby at 10:45?"

"Yes, that would be fine. I have some work to do, so I'll see you then."

At eleven sharp, Wo and Ka Kee arrived at the Committees office and were ushered into the conference room by the attractive granddaughter.

Walking down the hall, Ka Kee asked, "Does the attractive lady have a name?"

"My Ling," was the quick reply followed by, "Grandfather, Mr. Leung and Mr. Hoing are here to see you."

"Thank you, my child," and then continuing said,

"Gentlemen please be seated. Would you care for some hot tea?"

"No thank you Chairman, I just would like to see Comrade Hoing's work space and I wonder if you can provide him with a cell phone?"

"Certainly, and if you will follow me, Mr. Hoing's office is just down the hall."

The space was windowless, but well appointed with a desk, a big red leather couch and several side chairs along with a small conference table.

"I hope this office will meet your needs Mr. Hoing." Before Hoing could answer Ka Kee said, "Yes, this looks adequate. Does the building have twenty-four hour security?"

"Yes, we have electronic security as well as a full time night watchman."

"Well Wo, I guess this is your new home. I have a heavy schedule for the next few weeks, so if you need to get in touch with me just leave word at the hotel. I check in with the manager on almost a daily basis. Should an emergency arise, you can find me at this number."

Handing Wo his card, that contained no information other than a ten digit telephone number, he said in a low voice, "Add a two to each number to reach me."

Turning to the Chairman he said, "The 50 million is in the bank and ready to use. Comrade Hoing is the exclusive signatory on the account and he will fund any project that he deems necessary and reasonable. He is the final word, am I fully understood?"

"Yes, fully understood."

"Just one more point, no funds will be dispersed for any reason other than the purchase of property and the cost of any remolding that the property may require."

Chairman Wuhan was taken back by the penetrating eyes and the seriousness of the Generals words and stuttered, "Yes, General, I understand your requirements fully and in all cases Comrade Hoing will have the last word."

"Thank you both, and if questions come up you can leave word for me at the hotel and I will call you as soon as I am able."

Ka Kee turned, walked right past My Ling without so much as a glance and made the short walk to the Holiday Inn.

The two new associates looked at each other and in a shaky voice the Chairman commented, "He certainly knows what he wants."

Wo Hoing smiled and asked, "What is our first project comrade Chairman?"

CHAPTER TWELVE

The "Googleplex" in Mountain View, California, just fifty some miles from San Francisco, was a sprawling operation and home to the world's largest search engine. It and the New York facility were the master hubs and the very epitome of the information industry. In addition there were over one-hundred thirty-five other offices scattered around America from The Dalles, Oregon to Moncks Corner, South Carolina.

High on Ka Kee's "to-do-list" was a plan to disable all computer, phone, radio and television services within the first few hours of D-day. It would be a gargantuan task as there were twenty-three other search engines, over fifteen thousand radio stations, three-hundred and fifty TV stations, one-hundred forty-two thousand cellphone towers and another four hundred and fifty thousand small cell nodes across the country.

You could not blow them all up so there had to be another way. Early in the planning, Ka Kee and his staff created a select team of over one-hundred skilled technicians, all located in Mexico, that had been working on the problem for the past ten months. A Chinese electronic company fronted the operation and the employees were all Chinese Army personnel.

The team had come up with various solutions, but so far they had all been rejected as the man-power requirements were beyond the scope of possibility, there were just too many targets.

Solution after solution was put on the table, but so far they had all been rejected. Ka Kee sat on his penthouse veranda watching the sun sink into the Pacific Ocean, reading the latest reports from the project manager in Mexico, and it was not encouraging news.

THE ARMY WITHIN ZHANLUE

Siping his Kongsgaard Chardonnay, he wondered back inside, plopped down on a big comfortable couch, flipped on the TV and the big flat screen was filled with David Niven piloting his circa 1872 hot air balloon around the world.

It hit him like a ton of bricks. The winds from China eventually reach the west coast of America and then cross the country until they head out across the Atlantic Ocean.

He jumped up spilling his drink, and went running out to the railing to watch the sun sinking into the Pacific with the wind blowing in his face. Of course; balloons.

The project manager in Mexico was dumb struck when Ka Kee explained the operation.

"We blanket the skies over America with thousands and thousands of balloons, each carrying state of the art jamming equipment. We can impact the electrical grid, and every electronic product in America and we can also activate the kill switch in every chip that Taiwan has sent to America for the last ten years."

The project manager did not know that the prevailing winds swept across America from West to East but he did know that when Ka Kee was this excited and animated he better react. "I will assemble our team and explain your ideas Sir, and will get back to you shortly."

"Yes, you do that, and find the five best meteorologists in the Army and get them transferred to your command immediately. Understood?"

"Yes, Sir, fully understood."

Ka Kee sat down on the couch, picked up his I-pad and prepared to E-mail his mentor on a secure connection.

"Jet, please pull all stops to get a high altitude weather balloon launched from an aircraft carrier, off the coast of California. The prevailing winds should push it across America and the navigation equipment on board will give us constant readings of its exact location. If it had jamming equipment on board and if there were several thousand flying over America, we could disrupt all communications as well as activating all your Taiwan kill chips."

"Your student, Ka Kee"

Ka Kee finished off the bottle, set smugly watching the first wisps of fog roll in off the bay and congratulated himself on being so very, very smart.

Looking at his watch, and seeing that it was only a little after four, he hurriedly dressed, went down stairs, walked out of the hotel and down the street towards his dinner date.

He walked into the Committee of Eights plush quarters, moved across the room to the reception desk, looked down at My Ling and asked, "Would you please join me for dinner?"

The beautiful smile said yes, and they were soon installed at one of the back tables enjoying the very best that Scoma's and San Francisco had to offer.

CHAPTER THIRTEEN

It was almost eleven when My Ling's phone rang for the second time. She had ignored the earlier call, but now reached into her purse, extracted the device and curtly said, "Yes."

She listened for which seemed like a life time to Ka Kee, and finally said, "Yes, Grandfather, I am with Ka Kee and we are just finishing dinner. I'll be home shortly. Yes, Yes, Thank you."

"I'm sorry. You know how older folks worry?"

"No problem." he said, as he rose and came around the table to move her chair.

Walking out of Scoma's, past the parking valets, the smells of the wharf were powerful and yet when mixed with the fog and salt air made for a pleasing experience.

The dock area was alive with action as each fishing boat was getting ready to run the bay, slip under the Golden Gate bridge and race to the lobster grounds; either north or south of the narrow entrance to the greatest natural bay on earth.

My Ling and Ka Kee departed Scoma's in a taxi and were soon at the entrance to the Committee of Eight offices, which had her living quarters on the top floor.

"I would invite you up for a night cap but Grandfather frowns on such intrusions into his sanctuary."

"No problem. I will be traveling for the next ten days or so, but would like to see you again when I return."

"I shall look forward to that kind Sir," and turning quickly, she entered the door that the night watchman had been holding open.

Ka Kee walked back, up hill, to the Holiday Inn, vowing along the way, that he had to start limiting himself to just one bottle of his favorite Chardonnay.

CHAPTER FOURTEEN

Flight 336 from SFO to San Diego (SAN) is only an hour and thirty-nine minutes and the drive to Tecata takes about the same amount of time, depending on time of day and traffic.

Ka Kee pulled his Avis rental car into the parking lot at the El Ciclo Restaaurante a few minutes before his 11:00 lunch meeting with Mayor Ruiz.

As expected, General Lin Lau and the Mayor were waiting for their special guest to arrive and walked over to Ka Kee's car as he was setting the brake and closing up his briefcase, which had been open on the passenger seat.

"Good day", the jolly mustache said as Ka Kee exited the vehicle and Lin Lau added his greeting as well.

"How have you been Comrade," Ka Kee asked and the General replied, "Just fine Sir, just fine. Anxious for you to see the operation now that we are in high gear."

"Yes, I am looking forward to that."

Turning to the Major, Ka Kee asked, "Nice to see you again Mayor. I have been looking forward to lunch as I have tried other Mexican restaurants and none compare to Tecata's best.

The Mayor beamed, opened the door for his guests and immediately proceed down the hall to the private conference and dining room.

Turning to the owner, standing nearby, "Hector, there will just be the three of us today. Just bring us a pitcher of Margarita's made with Hiatus Tequila and a selection of your dishes of the day."

Ka Kee added, "Chile Relleno for sure, Hector."

Hector nodded 'Si' and hurried off to the kitchen.

As they were being seated Ka Kee asked, "Mr. Mayor have you received the export permits from the U.S Department of Commerce yet?"

"Indeed I have. Just came in two days ago. There are some minor requirements but nothing out of the unusual. "

Lin Lau asked, "Can you detail the requirements for me?"

"Of course. Pulling a small note book from his inside coat pocket, he flipped some pages and then said, "Yes, here are the requirements. One, each driver has to have a valid Mexican drivers license, Two, each container has to have a bolt seal, Model: Queenseal High Security lock and Three, there has to be a blue triangle decal, eighteen inches to a side on the front, rear and both sides of each container."

Looking up at his two companions he continued, "That's it."

Ka Kee smiled at Lin Lau and said, "Someone sure knows how to grease the wheels of industry."

They both laughed and the mustachio, not to be left out, contributed his quite loud belly laugh to the occasion.

The Major opened his ever present satchel type briefcase, made of hand-tooled Mexican leather, and handed Lin Lau the official government envelope that contained the details of the import license.

"You should have this for your files, just in case there is a hang-up with the U.S. Boarder Patrol."

"Thank you, Mr. Mayor, and now may I drink to your health." Picking up his margarita stein, he tipped the almost two handed vessel to the mayor and then to his superior.

Ka Kee was taken back. He had had margaritas before but nothing like this. "What is this stuff? It's fantastic."

"It's called Hiatus and it is made in a small distiller in Jalisco, Mexico which is near Puerto Vallarta on the Pacific Coast, and it's only sixty dollars a bottle."

"Are there more expensive tequilas?" Ka Kee asked.

The Mayor rolled his eyes and said, "Senior there is one called Clase Azul that sells for US$39,999.99 per bottle."

"No, that can't be right."

"Yes, Yes, Yes that is right, I swear on my Mothers grave."

"Well Mr. Mayor, I shall expect to sample that the next time I come to Tecata."

The Mayors eyes got as big as saucers and he stammered, "Yes, Sir I will try." The jolly mayor looked like he might burst into tears, at any moment.

Ka Kee laughed and said, "No need. I'm sure I like this better."

The major jumped up, refilled Ka Kee's stein, from the large pitcher and congratulated himself on dogging that bullet.

Lunch concluded when the pitcher ran dry and Hector was there to get another order but Ka Kee and the Mayor both waved him off.

The Mayor drove away from the restaurant and Lin Lau said, "Follow me to the warehouse."

The drive took less than twenty minutes and the quality of the road went from dogging Mexican pot-holes to a ribbon of new shinny black asphalt, once they were near the complex. The access road to the border patrol check-point was first class and Ka Kee smiled and thought to himself, "All it takes is money."

All hands came to attention as Ka Kee entered the facility. The troops were in awe of the Generals Leung's status and every uniform was inspection ready.

Ka Kee was introduced to each of the twenty high ranking officers in the organization and could tell from their demeanor that Lin Lau ran a very tight ship.

With the formalities over, Lin Lau lead him out into the warehouse and indicated he should be seated in the passenger seat of the bright-red golf cart.

The tour started with the uniform manufacturing area, moved on to the weapon assembly area where Ka Kee was able, at the test range,

THE ARMY WITHIN ZHANLUE

to fire the printed rifle and the hand gun. He was amazed that the units were so light and that they both used the same standard 9mm cartage. He was shown that none of the weapons would fire without a chip, in the handle, being activated by not only the ear tag, but by the identification cards included in each shipment.

Ka Kee could see that the racking, that covered the rest of the warehouse, was starting to fill up, according to the master plan.

Screeching to a halt, Lin Lau pointed out the huge map of America, on the north wall of the warehouse that had concentric circle lines radiating out from the Tecata warehouse. Each line represented two-hundred miles and the farthest point was the North tip of Maine, which was 2760 miles and thirteen circles from Tecata.

Lin Lau explained that as the deliveries were completed to the farthest-out circle, that is circle thirteen, that portion of the map would be over-painted with a transparent red paint. The next circle down, toward Tecata would be over painted with white wash and the next circle with a blue wash. When the map was completely red, white and blue washed the project would be done. On the west coast side of the map, each of the circle areas had a due date and Lin Lau, pointing to the dates said, "I guarantee we will make each date, Sir and as you can see, General, we will make the last deliveries into Southern California, Southern Texas and South Florida just months before D-day."

Ka Kee nodded understanding and looking at his subordinate said, "You have done an outstanding job here. President Hu and Jet How will so be advised."

"Thank you, General. Thank you."

Before departing the General reviewed the entire staff. He went down the ranks, pulled up to attention, and shook hands with each person, all three hundred. Upon completion of the review, he took a bull horn from the back of Lin Lau's golf cart and in Chinese told the staff.

"You are a small part of a very large puzzle. I know that you must wonder what is going on and how, what you are doing, will contribute to the mother land but I assure you that your names and your contribution will be remembered by your ancestors for centuries to come. In fact, everyone ridding this blue planet, from now until the end of time, will thank you for your service. A special medal has been designed, that I hope each one of you will wear proudly on your uniform, once this operation is over. The medal is a red, white and blue bar and every soldier, sailor and marine will know you are special when they see that decoration on your chest. Go back to work now, with renewed dedication, and with the understanding that your commanding officer, President Hu, knows and appreciates your service to the homeland."

Ka Kee, turned, saluted Lin Lau and said, "Thank you for your service. I will be back in several months to look at your map. Congratulations on a job well done."

With no more fan fare, he walked back into the office complex, down the hall, out the front door and headed his Avis car for the San Diego airport, satisfied that his 'Army Within' would have the equipment they needed to pull off the greatest invasion the world would ever see.

CHAPTER FIFTEEN

From the San Diego airport you could look across the beautiful harbor and see US fighting ships of all kinds, from aircraft carriers to tin cans, and everything in between, all tied-up at the Naval base on North Island.

The bay was home to the Pacific fleet which currently consisted of over sixty ships. The base covered 1600 acres of land, 326 acres of water and was supported by over 200 tenant commands that serviced the fleet.

Ka Kee could imagine the Chinese Communist flag flying over the bay and all the surrounding city and for the first time since Jet How had explained the project a wisp of doubt crossed his mind. Looking around the terminal at a cross section of the American population he had grave doubts that they would all give up, and meekly stand in a corner so their Chinese invaders could shoot them. No, no he thought, they will fight. The sailors of San Diego, their teenage sons, their parents, will fight. They will fight to the death to keep their homeland in tact, just like you would if the shoe was on the other foot.

His pensive mood stayed with him the rest of the day and well into the night, as he woke several times to find himself tossing and turning in his penthouse suite.

Morning on the veranda with steaming hot tea and a light breeze, trying to blow away the night time fog, was a special time and he could not shake the doubts that had been circling his brain for the last twenty-four hours.

Opening up his secure link on his I-pad, he found two messages that had just come in.

The first was from the commander of the garrison in Mexico City inquiring about the whereabouts of Captain Lee, who had not reported back to his unit since meeting with Ka Kee.

Ka Kee frowned and at first was concerned that the Captain might have met with an accident, but in retrospect thought, 'It's more likely that the demotion and the prospect of his returning to China, under adverse circumstances, made him flee. Yes, I would bet the farm he flew the coop, and that could be a danger to the whole operation. No telling what he might do. I should not have been so rash. Damn.'

Ka Kee composed a reply to the Mexican commander: 'Subject last seen at San Diego airport where he dropped me off for my flight back to San Francisco. Have no knowledge of his whereabouts. If he contacts me I will advise.

General Ka Kee Leung' The second secure e-mail was from his mentor.

> 'Student should know his solution is brilliant and all haste possible is being taken to make test happen within next two weeks. Staff additions are in transit to your neighboring country office.
>
> JHC'

'Well there is a feather in your cap', Ka Kee said out-loud, but inside his gut told him that the whole operation might have been breached by his rash behavior and he was almost sick to the stomach.

Setting on his veranda, sipping Chardonnay, he was suddenly cold and got up and went to the closet and pulled out a heavy sweater, which would feel good against the ever present breeze. As he set watching the weather go by, he was reminded of a line from one of Mark Twain's stories that went something like, 'The coldest winter I ever knew was a summer in San Francisco.'

Ka Kee smiled and thought, 'Samuel was spot on.'

Later in the day, after making travel arrangement for visiting county commanders in the Southern states, he called the Committee of Eight headquarters and the familiar voice answering the phone said, 'How can I help you Mr. Leung?"

"I will be leaving on another trip tomorrow and wondered if we might have dinner tonight?"

"I am sorry Sir, but I am attending the University of San Francisco and there is a special lecture tonight that I just cannot miss."

"Well of course not. I'll return in about a week so maybe we can have a rain-check until then? By the way, how is Mr. Hoing enjoying his job?"

"He seems to be working very hard, but I don't have much contact with him so I really could not say."

"Well have nice days, enjoy the lecture and I'll see you in ten days or so."

"Ka Kee, would you like to go to the lecture with me and then maybe afterwords we could have a light dinner? I will be leaving the office, by taxi about 4:30, if you care to ride along."

"I will be at your door at 4:30 sharp, and My Ling, I am looking forward to watching the education of a beautiful women."

At either end of the dead line smiles of anticipation crossed both faces.

The ride to the venue went fast and Ka Kee found himself in a dingy auditorium, part of a small group of twenty students, all of which looked like they had never had a haircut, that they had just rolled out of bed, put on the first clothes they had come to, lying on the floor, and somehow managed to get from their slum-quarters to the auditorium so they could listen to some wild-eyed professor scream about Victor Wolfenstein and his theories. It was depressing and Ka Kee could not help but wonder how this beautiful young girl could fit into this assembly of miss-fits.

The lecture imparted no information that interested Ka Kee and he could not wait for it to come to a close. Ninety minutes later, the torture finally ended, and when they were standing outside, and the long hairs were giving My Ling the once over, he asked: "Well wasn't that interesting?"

"Yes, I thought it was just marvelous. Hope I have the opportunity to hear him again. I just loved the part about workers being exploited by capitalistic system?"

"Do you have a favorite place you like to eat?"

"Not really."

"Well then, I am in charge."

Ka Kee hailed a taxi and told the driver, "Cliff House please."

"Yes, Sir. I'll have you there in jig time."

Leaning over to My Ling, Ka Kee asked, "What's JIG time?"

"Oh, he just meant it won't take long."

The Cliff House maitre d' fingered the hundred dollar bill and gushed them to the best window-table in the house.

The view was not good as the fog had already rolled-in but Ka Kee could have cared less.

Dinner was interesting. He learned a lot about the young lady while keeping his background shrouded in cliche's and generalities. She had no idea he was the third ranking officer in the Chinese Army and he had the feeling she would be shocked and dismayed if she knew the details of the diabolical scheme he was ramrodding.

As he watched and listened, he came to the conclusion that she certainly was beautiful, but just too young and inexperienced. He would have to find a more mature lady.

Ka Kee had the taxi drop her at the Committee office door and he came around the taxi, held her hands and said, "Thank you for a nice evening. Give your grandfather my regards. I am off to Florida tomorrow early but will call you when I get back."

With that said he hopped back in the taxi and left My Ling without even a brush of the cheek. She was disappointed, as she had planned to invite him up for a night cap, in that Grandfather was visiting relatives in San Jose. She had even set out a red silk nightgown, which would now return to the back of her closet, still unused. 'Men!' she thought as she followed the night watchman inside.

CHAPTER SIXTEEN

The trip to the south was uneventful. Ka Kee was able to meet with 43 county Commanders from tiny venues like Calhoun county, Florida (population 15,000) to Fulton county, Georgia with a population of over one million.

On the way home, he diverted to Bangor, Maine and made his way north to Aroostook County, the second farthest point North, in the 48 contiguous states, other than Angle, Minnesota, of course.

The county commander was rather portly for a Chinese but Ka Kee chalked it up to his occupation which was centered around the maple syrup industry. The state produces over half million gallons of the sweet goo every year and Ka Kee was going back to San Francisco with a large box of the sweet confectionery.

Ka Kee met his contact at a small town near the end of I-95 called Houton, not far from the New Brunswick boarder, and he had never experienced such hospitality. The commander's name was Fook So, and he had lived in Aroostook county for the past fifteen years. He had come into the country, illegally, across the Canadian border with his New Brunswick wife and he now had four sons. Fook was the last person Ka Kee would expect to be on board with the Zhanlue, but then life was full of strange bedfellows.

Fook wanted Ka Kee to come spend the night at his house and go out into the woods deer hunting. It was about all that Ka Kee could do to sidestep the insistence.

He finally shut down the invitations with a stern look and a reminder, "I am on a tight schedule and cannot accept your kind invitation. The reason I am here is to advise you that you and the other fifteen county commanders in Maine will soon be receiving your shipment of special merchandise, and I wanted to see where you plan to store these items."

Fook So, replying in a low measured voice said, "There is a new storage facility, just down the highway, and I have rented space there and paid for a year in advance, out of the funds that your office sent me."

"Good. Do you have any questions about the operation?"

"No, I understand that worlds are colliding and my heritage is very important to me so I shall follow my instructions to the letter and hopefully make my ancestors proud."

Ka Kee stood up, walked around the table and embraced his new friend and whispered in his ear. "You are the backbone of our country and your name will be known by all of our ancestors that will ever ride this blue planet. Thank you."

On the drive back to Bangor, he stopped and visited with four other Maine commanders and was pleased that they were all onboard, one hundred percent.

On the flight back to San Francisco, Ka Kee up dated his small notebook ledger. He had now visited 268 of the 3,143 counties and had to admit that it was an impossible task, to see them all. He would have to refine his list and concentrate on those counties that contained U.S. military bases or he would have to get some help.

On his I-pad he composed a text to Jet.

'Have covered 268 of 3143 counties. Need five line-officers, familiar with travel in America, to pick up the slack between now and when we march.

Do you have a launch date for Dragon?'

Your Student, Ka Kee'

The back bay was shrouded in fog, as the United flight from Boston slipped into SFO over the multi-colored salt flats. It was only 4pm which meant Ka Kee could look forward to dinner at Scoma's.

As he was waiting for his luggage, he called the Committee of Eight headquarters and was surprised when a male voice answered the phone.

"This is Mr. Leung may I speak to My Ling?"

"I'm sorry Sir, but she left for Hawaii yesterday."

"Hawaii?"

"Yes, I think she and several of her girl friends went for a week, but I'm not really sure of the exact time."

"May I speak to Wo Hoing please."

"Of course Sir, I'll put you through to his office."

"Wo Hoing here."

"Wo, can you have dinner with me tonight?"

"Of course Sir."

"Good, come up to the penthouse around six."

The line went dead. Wo pocketed his phone and mumbled to himself, "I will never get use to comrade Ka Kee."

CHAPTER SEVENTEEN

The next morning as Ka Kee was catching up on correspondence a short message came in from Jet.

Student, "Dragon" flies at 0500 hours, three days from now.'

JHC

Out in the Pacific the Chinese aircraft carrier, Liaoning, was steaming hard to reach their launch point within the next 72 hours. The destination was eight hundred miles Northwest of Hilo, Hawaii and six hundred miles off the coast of California.

The Liaoning started life as a Russian aircraft carrier named Varyag that the Chinese purchased in 1985. They tore it down, almost to the keel, and rebuilt the 999 foot giant over the next twenty-five years. It was commissioned in 2012 as the Chinese's first aircraft carrier. It is light years behind the likes of the USS Dwight D. Eisenhower (CVN-69), but that did not stop China from boasting about their new capabilities.

As the Liaoning steamed toward a pin-point in mid Pacific ocean the special contingent on board, from the China Meteorological Administration (CMA), were working 24/7 to put the finishing touches on the weather balloon, code named 'Dragon', and its payload that would soon be flying over America.

The data collection equipment consisted of standard meteorological equipment that would record temperature, humidity, wind speed, direction and atmospheric pressure. However, hidden within the computer control circuit boards were elements that would allow the operators to control altitude by radio signals, from the Chinese satellites, circling the globe.

As the helium/hydrogen filled latex balloon would rise to the 100,000 foot level (between 19 and 20 miles) special satellite controls could be activated that would let the operators, on board the Liaoning, control the altitude. Typical weather balloons do not have this capability but a Chinese team, of over two-hundred scientists, had worked 24/7 to develop this new control system.

The flight over America would be the first test of the system, and if it went wrong and crashed in Wyoming, the Chinese were certain that the Americans would not be able to penetrate the chips and find the altitude control circuit. To be certain, Jet suggested that they add a small explosive charge, to the package, that would activate when and if the balloon should descend below ten thousand feet.

Ka Kee was elated to hear the news and could not wait for the next 72 hours to pass. He needed something to occupy him and he had been putting off a trip to the Northwest, so he picked up the house phone and told the operator to connect him to the travel agent's office in the hotel lobby.

"Virginia this is Mr. Leung. Please book me on a United flight, early this evening, to Seattle. Yes, first class. I'll be down to pick up the ticket in an hour or so. And, Virginia, I will need a room at the Lotte Hotel for several nights as well. Thank you."

The population of Jefferson county Washington is thirty-three thousand, Snohomish county is 844,761, King county (where Settle is located) is 2,271,350 and Pierce county is 928,696. These were the four counties that Ka Kee chose to visit and each of the county commanders were apprehensive when they got the call from the General.

Ka Kee arrived too late to see any of the commanders but had reservations with each for the following day.

In his conversation with the King county commander, Ka Kee had asked for a restaurant recommendation and was told by the commander that he had heard that the Pink Door was a five star restaurant, but he didn't know if that was accurate.

It was accurate. The Italian food was outstanding and they even had a bottle of Napa Kongsgaard to go with the home made Potato Gnocchi, that was the best he had ever tasted outside of the Roveretto Hotel in Northern Italy.

Setting alone at the Mediterranean style bar, after dinner, he poured himself the last drippings from his dinner bottle and smiled to himself, and then congratulated himself, on being one of the luckiest men in the world. He lived and ate like a king, money was no object, and he traveled the world at will. He was best friends with the President of China's mentor, the famous Jet How Cheung, and he was the third highest ranking officer in the Chinese army and he was second in command of the greatest military zhanlue that the world would ever see.

A tap on his shoulder brought him out of the dream world and he turned to see a tall, dark haired gringo smiling at him.

"Excuse me Sir, but were you ever at a multi-nation military conference in Tokyo, at the Palace Hotel?"

Ka Kee's brain swirled around the question and without hesitation he answered, "Yes, 2014 or maybe 15, I believe, but how would you know that unless you were there as well?"

"I was there and we were seated next to each other for one of those boring speeches that high ranking officers think are important. I am John Hammon, Major at the time, but now retired."

"Well John, why don't you join me for a nightcap?"

"My pleasure Sir, and I am so sorry but I cannot remember your name."

"It's Ka Kee Leung and I too am retired. Do you live in the Seattle area John?"

"Well sort of. I have a home on a small island just South of Victoria Island, Canada. It is American soil, but only by a few hundred yards." he continued.

"Do you come here often?" Ka Kee asked.

"Yes, it's one of our favorite places and since my wife is visiting her parents, in Boston, and I had to be in the city it was a natural."

"What brings you to Seattle or do you live here?"

"No, right now I live in San Francisco and I just came North for a few days to visit some old friends."

"Is your schedule flexible?"

"Well tomorrow I have several appointments, but the next day is free."

"Why don't you come up to my island and we will take my 28' foot sloop out for the day. We can drag some hooks and maybe we will pick up a salmon."

"It's a date. Where shall I meet you?"

"Where are you staying?"

"At the Lotte Hotel."

"Nice up scale place. I'll pick you up there day after tomorrow at about eight, if your up that early."

"Of course and what's the dress for sailing?"

"Just causal and don't worry I have lots of heavy coats, on board, to keep you dry and warm."

"Thank you John. This is an unexpected pleasure and since I have never sailed much, I hope you can put up with me turning green. I understand the waters off the coast can be rather challenging."

"They can be but I have been doing it since I was fourteen so I think we will make the round trip with no fatalities."

John turned and exited the Pink Door leaving Ka Kee with a frown on his face. Thinking to himself as he finished the last inch, in the bottom of his Chardonnay glass, he wondered, 'How strange. I have been racking my brain and I just don't remember the man. Maybe it was one of those conferences where I drank too much.'

With the four county commander meetings behind him Ka Kee was looking forward to tomorrow and his adventure with John. He, however, had a nagging feeling and opened up his I-pad and sent a secure message to Jet.

> *'Jet, can you provide data on an American John Hammond who lives in Seattle, Washington area?'*
>
> *KKL*

Ka Kee was up at 5am and checking his E-mail found the following message from Jet.

> *'1. 'Student. Subject was major USA army, was intelligence expert on Asia and China.*
> *'2. Dragon flying should be overhead in 3 or 4 days.'*
> *Be careful grasshopper.*
>
> *JHC*

The BMW, 318i pulled up to the hotel at 8am sharp and Ka Kee went to the drivers side and said, "John, I didn't know how to contact you, but I am just feeling terrible and don't think I would make a good crew member today. If you will give me your number, I will call you the next time I am in Seattle and maybe we can make it happen. I'm really disappointed."

"Not to worry."

John reached into the glove compartment, extracted a standard business card and handing it to Ka Kee said, "Please do call me. Anytime. Hope you get to feeling better. Cheers."

"Damn," John yelled, as he merged into the boulevards morning traffic and immediately pulled into a 76 Union station, right next door. Screeched to a stop, he picked up his phone and made a hurried call.

"Pete, John. Well, he smelled a rat or he is sick. I'm not sure which. Any ideas?"

Pete; (Peter M. Duncan, Chief of National Threat Assessment Center in Washington, D.C.) "What a crock. Damn, I thought you would be able to get close to him but I don't know now. Did he give you a contact number?"

"No, so I can't just run into him in San Francisco, that would push the envelope way to far."

"Yes, Yes I agree. What now?"

"I'm grasping but maybe I can convert that girl at the Committee of Eight office."

"You think?"

"She seems so All American. Maybe I can just be a new friend, but if I ever bumped into Ka Kee, the shit would really hit the fan, for double sure."

"Your right, that's not even an option. We have to come up with something else."

"In the mean time, keep the tails on him and let me know if any brilliant ideas cross your pea-brain."

"Thanks boss, for the encouraging words."

A knock on the window brought John back to Seattle and he almost wet his pants. Ka Kee was the knocker and recovering from the shock, he rolled down the window and said, "Ka Kee, what's going on?"

"I watched you depart and then pull in here and I realized I had not given you a contact number."

"Yes, I was calling the Boat Works and telling them not to get the sloop out of storage because I would not be going out today."

"Well, here is my card. Call me anytime if you are down my way. I'll take you to dinner at a place on the wharf that will blow you away. Anyway I need to get back to the hotel before I throw-up on beautiful downtown Seattle."

John took the card and said, "Take care and I hope you get to feeling better soon."

"Me too." was the reply as Ka Kee turned and walked back up street toward the hotel.

John drove halfway back to his home, pulled over on an isolated street and called Pete.

"Pete."

"John here. You will never guess what just happened."

CHAPTER EIGHTEEN

The Threat Assessment Center had been tracking Ka Kee for only the last ten days and was firmly convinced that he was a special target, worth watching.

Ka Kee had come to the departments attention by a complete accident when one of their agents was on vacation in Cancun, Mexico. The agent was having lunch in a small beach front restaurant, near Ventura Park and as he left a red-eyed, scraggy looking Chinese man, setting on the ground near the entrance asked, "Sir could you spare a buck or two? I was robbed just after I got here and I'm flat broke."

"Did you inform the police?"

Standing up the man said, "Yes, but they just laughed at me."

The agent reached into his pants pocket, pulled out his money clip and pealed off a twenty, which he handed to the man. "Maybe this will help," he said as he headed for the beach. The money clip was a leather covered unit that featured a gold police star, and the Chinese man asked, "Are you an American law officer?"

The agent stopped, turned and said, "Why do you ask?"

"I saw the badge and I have some vital information that the USA government might be interested in paying me for."

The agent smiled at the derelict and said, "I doubt that you would have any information that would interest my government."

"How about a Chinese government plot to take over America?"

"And how, pray Sir, would you have such sensitive knowledge?"

"Up until ten days ago I was a Captain in the Chinese Army assigned to a unit in Mexico City. I made a big mistake and was immediately demoted and was scheduled to be sent back to China. I knew my career was over and that I might end up in a slave labor camp, so I left and decided to hide here. Unfortunately I was robbed the minute I got here and have been living on the street every since."

"Well Sir, that is an interesting story but I don't believe a word of it so hasta luego."

The agent turned and headed for the beach and the man shouted after him. "I can prove it, I can prove it. Just feel my ear."

Turning around the agent gave the man an incredulous look and said, "Feel your ear?"

"Yes, there is a computer chip inserted in my left ear lobe that lets the Army track me and almost everyone one of the Chinese illegals, coming over your southern boarder, has a similar chip. Feel!"

The agent walked back up to the man, reached up and could feel the chip between his first finger and thumb.

"Wait here!" the agent demanded as he walked a hundred feet away, dialed his superiors number in Washington."

"Pete here, what's going on Roger, I thought you were in Cancun on vacation?"

"I am and a big big plum just fell on me."

"Are you drunk?"

"No!, just listen please. So, I'm having lunch and...."

"Roger, take him to a local clinic, get the chip or whatever it is removed, and promise him anything he wants. Got it?"

"If it is a chip, I will cancel my vacation and hand deliver it to you either tomorrow or the next day. OK? I don't have much cash so will give him one of my credit cards."

"Sounds good Roger, and Roger I have a feeling it could be bigger than a plum. You are back on the clock as of right now. Good work, son."

"Thank you boss."

Walking back to the Chinese man, Roger said, "My name is Roger Pierce, who are you?"

"I am Dan Lee, Sir."

"Well Dan lets get you cleaned up and feed and then we will go get that chip removed so they can no longer track you. How's that sound?"

Tears rolled down Dan's cheeks as Roger guided him to a nearby taxi stand and told the driver, "Take us to the Hilton please."

Two hours later, after a shower, lunch and wearing shorts two sizes too big, Roger lead Dan into the International Medical Center, on Blvd Kukuikan, and said to the receptionist, "My friend has an ear problem and I would like to talk to the doctor in charge." A hundred dollar bill placed on the nice ladies desk brought an immediate response.

"Please follow me sir."

The ample hips moved down the hall to an examination room and the lady said, "Our Director, Doctor Lopez, will be with you momentarily."

"Thank you." Roger replied, as he indicated Dan should take a seat on the exam table while he stood near the door.

Within seconds, Doctor Lopez appeared and with a big smile asked, "Your friend has an ear problem?"

Roger smiled back, reached for his wallet, extracted his I.D. and credentials and handing them to him said, "Doctor I am with the United States government and Mr Lee is one of our undercover agents. He has a computer chip in his left ear lobe, that I would like removed, and then we shall depart and not bother you again. Five one hundred dollar bills were laid on a side table as Roger spoke.

The Doctor turned to Dan Lee and said, "Let me have a look."

After a brief exam, the Doctor looked at Roger and said, "Yes, its barley under the skin, but it should come out with no problem. There might be a little bleeding but nothing serious. Should I proceed?"

"Please do."

A few minutes later, with the chip in a small baggie and an equally small bandage on Dan's ear, the two men departed the clinic and taxied back to the hotel.

Once back in the hotel Roger said, "I am leaving this afternoon for home. You may stay here as long as long as you like and you may sign your name at any of the hotel shops for whatever clothes and toiletries you might need. In a few days you will receive a package with enough money to take care of your needs for the next six months. We may need you to come to Washington, and if so, I will send you the proper tickets and instructions. Is that agreeable?"

Dan nodded his head yes and meekly asked, "If I come to Washington will I be allowed to stay in America.?"

Roger smiled and said, "Of course, it is guaranteed. You have my word."

"Now, before I go I would like a run down on the job you had in Mexico City and what serious trouble caused you to go over-the-hill."

"I don't understand over-the-hill."

"What caused you to leave your post?"

"Oh, I understand."

Before Dan could continue Roger turned on a small tape recorder and said, "Hope you don't mind. It will help me give my superiors an accurate accounting of your story."

"No, that's fine. Well, almost a year ago I was transferred to a special division of almost two hundred and fifty officers that are now stationed in Mexico City."

"What was your job?"

"Well, because I speak English, I was assigned as a driver and courier. I escorted high ranking personnel from Mexico City, across the boarder to San Diego and other west coast cities."

"Who were these people?"

"Well the one that demoted me and told me I would be sent back to China was General Ka Kee Leung. I knew my life was over, so that is why I went over-the-hill as you say."

Roger did not recognize the name, but when the tape was played for his boss, all hell hit the fan.

Pete exclaimed, "My God, he is the third ranking officer in the whole damn Chinese army. What the hell is he doing in San Diego, sneaking across the boarder and visiting San Francisco? I want to know now, right now gentlemen!"

Within hours, most every person in the Assessment Center was on the job, and the full force and weight of the Federal government was being tapped to find the General.

Computer banks of every airline and every hotel were searched and data started coming in from every corner of the country. He was in Chicago, Maine, Florida, Georgia, San Diego and twenty three other American cities. Currently, he was renting the Penthouse suite at the Holiday Inn in San Francisco and spent time at a place called the Committee of Eight, a Chinese organization that helped Chinese immigrants find homes, in the Chinatown area of San Francisco.

Just yesterday, he flew to Seattle and is currently at the Lotte Hotel.

"Who do we have in Seattle?" Pete yelled.

"John Hammond," his assistant replied.

"Get John on the line, now."

"John, Pete at Assessment. Got a hot job for you and I mean hot."

"Sure Pete, I'm at your service."

"Ever hear of a Chinese General Ka Kee Leung?"

"Way back that name sounds familiar. I would have to think of it for awhile, why?"

"He is currently registered at the Lotte Hotel in Seattle. I want you to try to make contact with him and determine, what the hell the third highest ranking member of the Chinese Army, is doing in America."

"I will drive down there right now. Should be on station in an hour or so."

"Go!"

John meandered up to the consignee desk in the Lotte lobby and asked the nice looking lady, "I was suppose to meet a friend here. His name is Ka Kee Leung, Chinese of course, and I have rung his room but there is no answer."

"Seems to me, Yes, a Chinese gentlemen asked me for a restaurant recommendation and I told him about the Pink Door, which is just down the street. I remember his eyes lite up and he said, 'Yes, Pink Door, that was the place one of my friends recommended'. That was maybe an hour ago Sir, so he is probably still there."

"Thank you very much. You have made my day."

CHAPTER NINETEEN

The E-mail from Jet was short and to the point.

'Dragon hitting west coast near Tillamook, tonight at around ten pm your time.'

JHC

Ka Kee would be arriving in San Francisco shortly and he was still, frowning his brow, over the incident with John Hammond. 'Was it really just a chance meeting or had the Americans gotten wind of the zhanlue?' He could not help but wonder.

If he had asked the attractive lady sitting in the last row of first class, Special NTA agent Susan Loveless, she might have been able to set his mind to rest.

It was nice to be back in San Francisco again and standing on his top floor veranda, sipping his drink of choice, high powered binoculars, just across the street, manned by NTA agents could read his lips. The only other suite, on the Holiday Inn's top floor, was now being occupied by Susan and a San Francisco based team of six NTA agents.

"Pete, Susan Loveless here. 'Chip', (Ka Kee's new code name) is back at home base, we have an observation unit across the street and I, and a team of six, are installed in the penthouse next door. Any special instructions?"

"No, just do it by the book and pay close attention to his daily contacts and set up shadows, if you think it is necessary. Sue, use all the resources you need. We have to break this as soon as possible."

"Roger, and Sir, I was wondering if you have you been able to break into his phone and E-mail yet?"

"Negative, the lab guys tell me it's something they have never seen. They will keep trying, but without the unit I really don't think we will be able to crack that nut."

"Sir, how shall I weave Hammond into this or just let it takes its natural course?"

"I'm not sure. If he canceled the sailing trip because he smelled a rat, it will be hard to bring John back into the mix, however, if he contacts John then the doors wide open. Make sure you keep John in the loop and since Ka Kee gave him his number we may be able to use that contact later, we will just have to wait and see."

"Yes, Sir, anything else?"

"No, just enjoy San Francisco. There is a little bar on Columbus street called the Gold Spike that has Italian food to die for."

"I'll keep that in mind, and Pete, thanks for giving me the reins on this. I know it's critical and I will be on it 24/7.

"Your welcome young lady."

CHAPTER TWENTY

Ka Kee stood out on his roof top veranda and looking north smiled, the Jet How Cheshire-cat smile, as he visualized the Chinese balloon floating over the Oregon coast, maybe right over Three Arch Rocks, off Oceanside or down the coast, across the Oregon Beach Dunes near Florence. Let's see, he thought, 'It should clear the Cascades, might drop a little south, past Boise and head out over southern Wyoming and the northern Rockies.'

He walked back in the living room, picked up his lap top and punched in 'USA map'.

The unit reacted with a colored map of the North American continent. He traced, with his finger the imagined route, before the balloon would finally sail off the continent, and be told to fall into the Atlantic Ocean. Chinese war ships would be waiting to retrieve the instrument package, provided the kill switch on the explosive charge could be turned off. As he walked back on the veranda, looking up at the night time sky, he thought, 'It was all so simple', and then he said out loud, "Damn, I should have bet Jet that the Americans would never even know it was in their air-space." Looking around he smiled to himself and thought, 'Well it's not over. It may take a week or even ten days to cover three-thousand miles, so I'll just have to wait and see how good the American air defense system really is.

The NTA team, across the street, recorded Ka Kee's time on the veranda and when the video was played for Director Duncan, he asked the technicians, "Did I hear that right? Did he say the Americans would never know it was in their air-space?"

The three technicians, who could all read lips. nodded yes, as the Director picked up the phone and dialed the private number of the FBI Director.

"Christopher, Pete Duncan at NTA. Sorry to bother you but we have an intercept that indicates a foreign power may be trying to penetrate our West coast air-space. Is it possible for you to get the military cracking on this, it could be important?"

"Of course, Pete, send me the source docs, to the same number you just called, but change the last digit to seven. I will get back to you as soon as I have any data from the military."

"Thanks Chris, I'll send a backup report through regular channels."

"Any time, Pete."

With the full staff gathered around, Pete asked, "Does anyone have any bright ideas on what the General might have been referring to?"

Bill, one of the older staff members said, "I did research on the Tiananmen Square incident, that happened in 1989, and the guy who put down the riots was an army officer named Jet How Cheung. The current President of China owes his reign to crushing that rebellion so its possible Mr. Jet still has his finger in the pie."

"Fantastic Bill!, Your new job is to track Mr. Jet and bring me all the information possible. If you need help, select a crew and get with it."

"Yes, Sir. In 24 hours I'll tell you what the gentleman eats for breakfast."

Almost good to his word, Pete was reading Bill's report twenty-eight hours later and was amazed. Jet How Cheung was probably the second most powerful man in China, after President Hu, of course. He held no official post, but was the Presidents personnel friend and maybe mentor. He had been involved in every evil program that the Chinese government had undertaken, in the last thirty years, and his fingerprints were all over the upset win of Biden over Trump in 2020. There was documented information that Jet had given Black Lives Matter huge sums of money to help defeat Trump and that he had organized and funded Chinese student groups, at almost every

American college or university, to work toward defeating Trump. Bill had inserted a side bar: (Note: There were over 370K Chinese students enrolled in US colleges in 2019.) Recently, Jet had built a villa on a small island off the Chinese coast and one report said he had received one-hundred million US dollars as a retirement bonus. He likes rice cakes for breakfast.

Pete Duncan called Bill into his office and said, "Nice report, keep digging, we need to know everything about Mr. Jet and look into his travel as well. Was he in America before the 2020 election, if so where? You know where I'm going, Bill, so just follow it wherever it leads you. Great job."

"Thanks boss."

Pete's phone rang as Bill was leaving and the boss said, "Pete here."

"Pete, Chris; guess what?"

Surprising Chris, Pete replied, "There is an unidentified high altitude weather balloon in our air-space."

"How in the hell did you know that?"

"Just an educated guess."

"Well you are right. It's over the Rockies now and I am getting Presidential authority to shoot it down." As an after thought Chris asked, "Does your crystal ball tell you where it's from?"

"Of course, it's Chinese and Chris you might tell the President where it's from and see how that impacts his decision."

"What do you mean Pete?"

"Just a hunch, a far out hunch, that's all."

"I'll let you know and for now the press has not picked this up and we hope it stays that way, capisco?"

"Yes, I got it Sir."

The lines went dead and both men had the same thought. 'What will Biden do when he finds out it's Chinese?'

CHAPTER TWENTY-ONE

Ka Kee was at SFO, waiting for a Southwest flight from San Diego to arrive, with his five new assistants. They had been smuggled across the border by a courier, from the Mexico City office, that had replaced Dan Lee.

Walking up to the group, Ka Kee said, "Gentlemen, I am your new employer, please get you luggage and meet me out front."

With no more ceremony, he turned and walked outside and stood next to a big limousine that would take his new employees to the Holiday Inn.

The new employees scurried off to claim their bags, none wanting to be the last man to keep the General waiting. They were all apprehensive about this assignment; after all, the boss was the third highest ranking officer in their army and a screw up wold mean the end to their career.

Installed in the limo, Jet asked, "Have I met any of you before?" And then quickly adding in a serious tone, that got the listener's full attention. "We only speak English!"

No one answered the question.

"Well, some say I am not easy to get along with, but if you follow instructions, to the letter, you will all return home with your careers in tact and maybe a special citation."

Handing the man, seated next to him, a small note book he said, "Name, rank, last assignment, and experience traveling outside of the motherland."

Ka Kee had, of course, already received an e-mail resume, on each of the officers, along with a photo, but it was going to take awhile to put a face with a name.

"Who is senior among you?" The man setting next to him replied, "My colleges are Majors and I am a Colonel, so that would be me Sir."

"And your name?"

"Colonel He Ping."

"Have you traveled America He?"

"Yes, Sir. I attended Princeton for three years and did graduate work at Stanford, in California, for two years."

"Good. You will be directing your staff on a daily basis" and making eye contact with each of the officers, seated in the limo he added, "and orders you give will be carried out with efficiency and speed."

"Yes, Sir."

"When we arrive at the Holiday Inn, which is in the heart of San Francisco's Chinatown, you will each register, go to your rooms and unpack, and then come up to my quarters, which is the Penthouse West. We will go to an early dinner, so you can all catch up on your sleep. Tomorrow morning, please be in my quarters by 0800, where breakfast will be served. Questions?"

After dinner and after his new charges had been dismissed, Ka Kee was setting on the veranda, with his ever present glass of Chardonay, reviewing his note book.

Speaking softly to himself he said, "Colonel He Ping, Major's Wang Jianwu, Yang Xuejun, Zhang Youxia and Zhou Yaning."

Picking up his I-pad, he reviewed the resumes and concentrated hard on putting a face with a name. Satisfied with his memory work he finished his glass, went inside, took a quick shower and hit the rack.

His new group seemed all bright eyed and eager as they enjoyed an American breakfast of bacon, eggs and toast and the NTA guys, across the street, could almost smell the bacon.

"Wonder who they are?" Pete said, and Bill piped up, "They all have a military bearing and there seems to be a pecking order, so my moneys on military officers. I have a list of their names, which Susan got from the hotel staff, and we are running them through the computers now.

One of Bills crew came rushing into Pete's office and handed him a note.

"Mystery solved. Let's see we have four Majors and one Colonel. The Colonel attended Princeton and Stanford and is stationed in the Northwest Region as a Western Analysis Officer, whatever that is. I'll have data on each Major before the day is over Sir."

"Thank you Bill, great job, now can anyone tell me how these five got into the country?"

One staffer added, "Well they all came into SFO from San Diego, so I guess it was Beijing, Mexico City, Tijuana, a short walk across the border, and then Southwest to SFO."

"Looks that way," Pete agreed and then added, "We were a hell of a lot safer when Trump was building the wall and Kamala wasn't the boarder czar."

Heads nodded around the room and Bill offered, "If he gives them instructions, on the veranda, we will get every word."

"Let's hope," Pete offered.

Ka Kee had eaten before his quests arrived so he was free to sip his tea and get acquainted with each man. Most of the conversations were recorded by the spooks across the street, and within hours, that combined with Bill's searches were giving the NTA staff a good picture on who they were dealing with. All five had attended colleges in America and some had lived in the states for as long as six years. They were all from different parts of China but had one thing in common. They were all Foreign Intelligence officers, were all attached to foreign intelligence gathering units, all spoke English, all had been educated in American colleges or universities, and they were all from families that had ties to the countries leadership elite.

Pete observed, "They certainly are an impressive group. Does anyone have a guess as to why they are here?"

Silence greeted his request and then Bill said, "Sir, Chips has been traveling the country, going to out of the way spots and visiting with Chinese nationals. I have a feeling he needs help and I will bet the farm we see these guys, fanning out all over the country, doing exactly what he has been doing. He just needed more horses."

Pete weighted the insight and asked rhetorically, "What's the point. Why? What's the end game?" It has to be important, otherwise, Ka Kee would not be involved." Looking around the room he added,"Boys and girls, we have to find out why. In view of the Chinese weather balloon flying over America, coupled with the gang of five showing up, something big is in the works and we must find out what. I truly believe it is now a question of national security."

Grim looks intimated from everyone in the room.

Pete added, "Tell Susan to put operation 'George' in high gear. Assign teams to each of the Gang of Five. I want to know everything they do and I mean everything. Capiche?"

The troops scattered and Pete picked up the phone and called John Hammond in Seattle.

"Yes, Pete."

"John, this is beginning to look big time. I think it's a major plot in the making. I am sending you a secure file on where Ka Kee has been traveling. See if you can come up with any independent patterns, something we are overlooking. If you see something, get on your horse and check it out yourself. Report only through me and John, spare no expense, regardless of where it might take you."

"Thanks for the confidence, Pete. I will be on it 24/7."

Several hours later, filtering through the file Pete had sent by e-mail, John asked himself, 'Why San Diego? He has been there twice. What's the draw, other than the Pacific Fleet headquarters and the border. Does it tie in with the Mexican office that Dan Lee was working for? Where was that, Yes, Mexico City.'

John picked up the phone and dialed Pete's number.

"Pete here, what's up John?"

"When Ka Kee was in San Diego did he rent a car, and if so, how many miles did he put on the vehicle?"

"I'll get back to you shortly."

Pete stuck his head in Bill's office and said, "When Chip went to San Diego did he rent a car and if so how many miles did he put on it?"

"I'm on it boss."

Three hours later, John's phone rang, "Yes, Pete here. He drove the Avis rental 272 miles."

John, thought out loud, "That means he went 136 miles from the airport. Draw that circle on your map and see how far into Mexico that goes. Send me a copy."

"You got it," Pete replied.

The map showed that the only real town within the 136 mile radius was Tecata, Mexico.

"Pete, John. How about an aerial map of the circle with concentration on the Mexico side of the border. Any new construction, any new roads, anything that has changed in the last 9 to 12 months."

"We are on it, John."

It was almost midnight, when John's phone rang.

Pete started out, "Sorry to bother you this late, but I couldn't wait until morning. The largest warehouse in Mexico is a few miles outside Tecata and it was just finished a few months ago. There is a new road from the complex to the border, and they even built a new freeway on-ramp and border station on our side, but the kicker is State Department issued a permit to the City of Tecata to import almost 6000 containers with special permits that allow the containers to cross the border with no inspection, provided the truck drivers have a Mexican license, and there are blue triangles on all sides of each container."

"6000 containers?"

"Yes."

"What's in the containers."

"The permit says 'General Merchandise'."

"Who in the hell approved that?"

"The instructions, to State, came directly from The White-house."

"What?"

"You heard me correct, and John, I see Hunter's finger prints all over this, so we have to proceed with extreme caution."

"I am blown away, but I have another question."

"What's that?"

"Why would Ka Kee go to Manteno, Illinois, which is south of Chicago on I57?"

"I don't have a clue?"

"I do."

"Well, spill the beans."

"The Chinese are building the largest battery factory in the world. It will employee 2600 Illinois farmers and they received a $536 million dollar tax credit from the State of Illinois. Pete, I'll bet you the farm, the State Department is up to their ass in this and based on what we learned today, I bet the White-house had a hand in this deal as well."

"John, this is getting hairy. I really appreciate your input. What's your next move?"

Thought I would go down to that new border control stations and look for blue triangle container trucks, and then follow one. Haven't been on a road trip for awhile. It will be a pleasant break. With your approval, I'll call you along the way."

"John, follow your nose and be careful. I have a feeling these guys are playing for keeps. Do you want any backup or company?"

"No, I think I can handle it and Pete, thanks for getting me in the mix."

"No sweat, John."

CHAPTER TWENTY-TWO

John was dressed in faded Levis, leather jacket and a red Diamond-Back's baseball cap, as he sat on a bench outside the border control station near Tecata. He had established his government identity with the boarder chief and had been watching the action for the last several hours. It was now near eight in the evening and the traffic was light, however, several containers, with the blue triangles, had cleared the station, in just the last twenty minutes. They had all headed east on Cal. 94. He assumed correctly, that they would access I-8, go east to Yuma and then head north on Cal. 95 and eventually interline with I-80 at Needles.

One of the border agents flopped down beside him and said, "It sure is sweet duty out here. I usually draw the Tijuana crossing and its gangbusters 24/7."

"Have you ever seen any of the containers with the blue triangles go west?"

"No. they all go east." Pausing, he added, "Sure is strange that we don't have to inspect those triangle units. Never saw anything like it in my eighteen years on the border."

"How many would you estimate pass through here a day?"

Removing his hat and scratching his ample red hair, he replied, "Maybe ten or twelve a-day. Eh, at least a dozen."

"Any idea where the come from?"

"Sure. The biggest damn warehouse in Mexico. It's just huge. Me and the misses visit her relatives, south of Tecata, and we saw it, a few months back, and Mister, it's not only big but it is surrounded by two cyclone fences, each with that razor wire on top. Nobody's breaking in there, that's for sure."

"Well, thanks for your hospitality. Guess I'll hit the road."

"Going to Diego?"

"No, think I'll head east."

"We'll have a good trip."

John unwound from the bench, meandered over to his Avis SUV, and set the GPS for Yuma.

Driving around a Pilot Truck stop, in Yuma, after the two hour drive from Tecata, it was easy to spot the quarry. No need to follow one particular unit and take the chance of the driver noticing the tail.

It was almost eleven when John pulled into the Best Western, on South Castle Dome Avenue, in Yuma, for a few hours shuteye.

John had just finished his breakfast, at the Yuma truck stop, and was sitting in his car, deciding how to proceed when one of the blue triangle rigs pulled out right in front of him, heading for I-8. He followed along for a few miles, but soon became bored with the sixty-five miles per hour speed, so he put the hammer down and was in Needles, California just four hours later.

The first truck stop on the edge of town only had three triangle units in residency. This was going to be a slam dunk, maybe he should just take I-40 to Albuquerque and then turn north on I-25, and he could be in Denver the day after tomorrow, 'Or stupid,' he said out loud, 'you could just drive up to Vegas, spend a few days at the Bellagio, and fly to Omaha.' Continuing his talking with himself, 'I'll bet the farm, I can find a triangle unit, at a truck stop on I-80, outside Omaha.'

Most of the passengers on the Southwest flight from Las Vegas to Omaha were tight lipped, grim faced Nebraska farmers, that had lost their ass in the city that never sleeps. John, smiled to himself, recalling that he walked out of the Bellagio four thousand dollars richer, thanks to a poker machine that gave him a royal flush just minuets before departing.

The Omaha airport is at Eppley Field and it is built along side the Missouri river. It was easy for John to find his way onto I-80, across the water-way, and pulling into the Pilot station outside Council Bluffs, Iowa, his luck held as four blue triangle trucks, were in residence. That sure beats driving 1300 miles, he thought to himself.

Out of the four, he selected one being pulled by a big red Peter Built tractor unit to shadow, and said out loud, "Take me to your leader, please."

The Peter Built merged onto I-80 east, and in Des Moines turned north on I-35. Two-hundred and fifty miles later, it pulled into a suburb of Minneapolis, called Coon Rapids, and from a truck stop, on the outskirts of town, John watched the driver make a phone call.

Within fifteen minutes an old, dark green, Range Rover pulled up beside the big red Peter Built, and a small oriental man indicated the driver should follow him.

The truck followed the Range Rover to 9900 Vale Street, Northwest. The Range Rover's driver hastily parked on the street, got out and directed the truck to back up to one of the larger storage units, in the complex, where four other oriental men were waiting to unload the trailer.

John drove past the storage unit and parked on a side street a block away. He walked back, and from a secure vantage point, watched the five orientals, use a bolt cutter to remove the Queenseal lock from the container and within an hour, approximately 296 cardboard boxes had been unloaded into the storage unit.

The Mexican driver, taking a siesta in his truck, was awakened by the Range Rover driver, who banged on the truck door. "Si Senior," the driver said from the open driver-side window. "We are done unloading. You are good to go."

As the Peter built disappeared down Vale avenue the leader locked the storage unit, the four helpers piled into a nearby station wagon and the leader returned to the Range Rover parked on the street. The whole operation had not taken two hours.

When the unloading was almost complete John returned to his vehicle and moved it to a parking place across the street from the storage unit. He was able to get both vehicle license numbers and immediately phoned them into Pete's office. No use following either one of them he thought, the plates will give us verse and chapter.

An hour later, as John was lying on the bed at the Best Western White Bear Country Inn in nearby Blaine, Minnesota, his phone rang.

"Hi Pete, what have you got?"

"I have sent you an E-mail with data on two of the five. Will have full details on the driver of the Range Rover and the driver of the station wagon, but cannot identify the others at this point. John, I am going to send a team from our Minneapolis office to put this to bed. How many boxes do you think there were?"

"My rough count would be close to three-hundred"

"Where they all the same size?"

"Yes, as far as I could tell. They looked to be about two foot square and about that high."

Off phone, John heard Pete asking, "Bill, how many cubic feet in 40-foot container? Seconds later Bill replied,"2350."

Pete continued, "Two by two by two is eight cubic feet. Eight into 2350 is what?" Bill's reply, "293 boss."

"Well John, your three-hundred count was close. Congratulations."

"What's the plan, Pete?"

"You, my man, need to get a good nights sleep. Drive to Minneapolis tomorrow and get a flight to Seattle. Your road trip is over except for one last job."

"What's that?"

"Before you drive to Minneapolis, go to the storage unit, confirm the space number where the boxes were stored and try to rent a unit on either side, if possible. If not, rent one as close to the unit as you can. If you need a cover story just tell them you have a friend, that needs some extra storage for his business.

"I suppose your going to have a team from Minneapolis have all the fun?"

"Right on. Get some rest and we will take it from here."

"And John, job well done."

"Thanks, Pete."

CHAPTER TWENTY-THREE

Pete cleared the call with John and yelled at his assistant, "Get everyone to the conference room, now!"

Over thirty bodies were cramped into the conference room, each with a look of anticipation and there was a foreboding atmosphere, to the gathering.

"We, ladies and gentlemen, have a decision to make that will stretch us all to our individual limits."

You could have heard a pin drop on the moon.

"About a dozen of these blue triangle trucks are coming across the border every day and if they all follow the format that John Hammond just exposed, there will be 6000 storage units, around the country, filled with whatever the transported goods may be. We know it will be near the 6000 number as the import permit, given to the Tecata mayor, specified that number. Within the next twenty-four hours, we shall break into the storage unit in Coon Rapids and determine exactly whats in the boxes, but in the meantime; today, twelve other storage units will fill up and we don't have a clue where they are. Twelve more will fill up tomorrow and thirty days from now there will be 360 more storage units, and as I said, we don't have a clue where they are, nor do we know how many have shipped before we got wind of the operation."

Looking around the cramped space Pete continued, "The sixty-four thousand dollar question then becomes, do we put a tail on every trailer?"

Bill, broke the silence. "Sir, I don't think we have any choice, and if that means calling in the FBI, the Army and the Marines, then we need to do it and do it now. Every day we loose twelve sites."

"That's right Bill. What say the rest of you?"

Consensus welled up to support Bill and Pete said, "OK, put together a schedule of every field agent and every employee that can assist. We will need 360 agents to cover the next thirty days, however if the average tail takes five days then each agent can make at least five trips per month. Bill, pick a staff, drop everything else and get us a manning schedule before the day is over. Can do?"

"We will give it a go, boss."

"Meeting adjourned."

Pete returned to his office and called John.

"What's up Pete?"

"If you want to go back to Omaha and pick up another blue triangle to tail, please do so. I'm organizing a task force to follow every container and it may be in place as early as tomorrow morning. We are pulling all stops and shelving all other operations. This is job one!"

"Sure Pete," then adding, "I will get on it as soon as I rent the storage unit. I was just leaving to go there now so I should be back to you with the storage units number and details about the unit I rent."

"Thanks John."

Before Pete could hang-up John added, "I'll bet you a steak dinner I can find a triangle in Minneapolis."

"You're on," Pete said, as he looked up to see Bill hurrying into his office.

"Boss, the field office in LA has dispatched eleven of their agents to the Tecata border station and the operation will start yet today. What shall we call it?"

"Pete stared out his window, at the Washington Monument, and replied, "'Operation George'. Now get the hell out of here and start tailing something."

Minutes later secure communications alerted every field office that 'Operation George' had commenced and it carried the highest treat level possible, Level Seven, which was code for 'Imminent Foreign Incursion'

Bill stood in Pete's office door and informed him, "LA office covering today, San Francisco tomorrow and Seattle the day after. By then, I should have ten teams scheduled and we will rotate them every four or five days, as you can get from Tecata to Maine, even in an eighteen wheeler, in about four days."

"Let me see the master schedule, when you get it printed out, and Bill, we will need a master list of each storage facility by state."

"Roger, Boss."

Before Bill took a step Pete said, "Bill, delay that. On second thought give me an alphabetical list of counties by state. I am thinking maybe this is a county by county operation. How many counties are there?"

Bill consulted Goggle, on his phone, and replied, "3143 in the country, Boss."

Pete smiled and said, "I'll bet you the farm, Bill, that we will find one storage unit per county."

CHAPTER TWENTY-FOUR

"Pete, the boxes are in unit fourteen and I rented fifteen next door. I told the manager that a friend of mine would be putting a lock on it later in the week. Off to Minneapolis to earn a steak. Bye."

Pete smiled as he put down the phone and thought of the fishing trip that he had been on with John earlier in the year. Nothing regular, that's for sure. The boat was a sea plane with no doors. John flew it into secluded bays, that dotted the landscape, along the coast of Vancouver Island, Canada. He swore he had a Canadian fishing license, but when a Canadian fish and game boat appeared, on the horizon, lines were quickly cleared and 'Old Glory', the 1949 Piper float-plane, was up and away. 'What a guy,' Pete thought.

The Chicago NTA office was run by an old hand, named Terry Pinzon, who was currently in a deep conversation with the NTA Director.

"So that's the big picture as of right now Terry. We have to find out what's in the boxes, for now, just one will do. They are all identical in size, so I am assuming they will have similar contents. At any rate we have the buildings drawings and the inside walls are 29 gauge corrugated metal sheets. I don't think they will miss one box so you will need to cut an opening about three foot square. The engineers recommended that you cut the hole near the ceiling so you can remove one of the boxes from the top of the stack."

"Pete, any means we use to cut the hole will generate heat and we could start a fire, after all they are cardboard boxes that can easily ignite."

"You are right, of course. Any other suggestions?"

"Well, we could fill our unit with all manner of electronic equipment and then a bunch of criminals might rob our unit, as well as several neighboring units. I think the local police might even be able to help us with the ruse."

Pete replied, "That's why we hire old guys like you. Get it going, we need that robbery to happen, soon."

Two trucks from the Micro Center in Chicago, one of the biggest electronic stores in the state of Illinois, arrived at the storage facility on Vale street, in Coon Rapids, the next day, and unloaded box after box of electronic equipment. Everything from big flat screens to cell phones and everything in between. The manger of the complex watched the unloading and was surprised that the gentleman, that rented the unit, had not used the Micro Center name. When asked about that, one of the truck drivers said, "Oh. Mr. Hammond is one of the owners and he usually does what he wants."

Satisfied, the manger returned to his office and within a few hours the transfer of goods was completed, there was an Ace hardware lock on the door, and the robbery would take place in just a few days.

"Pete, John here. I just followed a triangle to Corcoran, Minnesota, which is in Hennepion county, a suburb of Minneapolis. They are unloading at a storage facility at 7340 Fir Lane North. You owe me a steak."

"Boxes, again?"

"Right on, brother. I'm going to see if I can find one more and then I'll head back to Omaha. I am going to have the biggest most expensive steak in Omaha at The Stockyards Steakhouse. Have you been there?"

"No, John I have not."

"Well, you need to get out more. Get in that private jet of yours and come help me."

"How many more are you going to case?"

"I'll see what I find, at the truck stops on I-80, and Maybe by this time, day after tomorrow, I will have several more addresses for you.

How's it going on getting your hands on one of those boxes in Coon Rapids?"

"The robbery is scheduled for Friday."

"Who in the hell thought of that?"

"That old fart, Terry Pinzon in Chicago."

Before the line went dead Pete heard, "That smart old SOB."

Before the robbery, on Friday night, John had tailed three more trucks and the same modus operandi played out at each final destination. Bill took note that each delivery, within a particular state, was to a different county. 'Pete was right,' he thought.

Saturday morning found the green Range Rover setting outside the office, of the storage unit, and one mad Chinese man yelling and screaming at the local police and the manager. The locks on 14, 15, 7 and 4 had all been cut with a high powered bolt-cutter and while most of the merchandise in 15 was gone, nothing seemed to have been taken from units 4, 7 and 14. The contents in 4 and 7 had been tossed about and several boxes of clothing had been opened and scattered about in 14 but other than that it was only 15 that had suffered a big loss.

The police captain took the Chines-man aside and said,"I know your upset, but it does not look like they took any of your merchandise, so why don't you just pack it back up and go get a new lock. We will let you know when we find those responsible."

Ka Kee's commander of Anoka County Minnesota agreed and headed for the hardware store to get a new lock. He didn't think to count his inventory so he had no idea that two boxes were missing. The ruse had worked and Pete called Terry to congratulate him on a job well done.

The boxes arrived by private jet at NTA's lab and Pete, Bill and several others were there for the opening.

Each box had a unique bar code label that was followed by a sir name, in Chinese and in English. There were no other markings on the box.

The lead technician asked, "Time to open Sir?"

"Yes, time to open."

Before running a box cutter down the taped seal he said with a diabolical smile, "We scanned it Sir and I guarantee there is no bomb inside, so rest easy."

Pete smiled back as the technician cut the tape and opened up the lid. A single sheet of paper, in a plastic sleeve, had instructions in English on one side and Chinese on the other. Another plastic sleeve contained two identification cards complete with picture, name, rank, and name of county commander.

Setting the instruction aside, he then removed three complete uniforms. Socks, pants, shirts with insignia's and a standard baseball cap, with more insignia's. The pants and shirts were standard military tan as was the cap. Wrapped in clear plastic bubble wrap were two plastic guns. One, an AK-47 look alike and the second a standard looking hand gun. Instructions, both in Chinese and English showed how to assemble the long gun and how to activate each, with the I.D. cards, after the cards had been placed within an inch of the recipients ear chip.

Pete and the assembled crew were almost speechless.

Pete finally said, "Gentlemen, the State Department of the United States of America issued an import license for 6000 containers, each with about 300 such boxes or," Looking at Bill for help, while Bill was pushing buttons frantically, on his I-phone and then Bill held the answer up for Pete to see, "1.8 million such boxes. That means 3.6 million fire arms." With his voice trailing off he said, "If each gun just killed one American, well you get the picture. These boxes are as highly classified as I can make them. You will be under extreme penalty if you breath one word of this outside this room."

Looking around the room with a sad forlorn look he continued, "Someone in our government is behind this and right now I don't have a clue. We cannot share this information until we determine WHO."

Pausing and picking up the plastic hand gun, he looked at the assembled group and said, "This was designed to kill our fellow citizens and we know now that there are at least 1.8 people, in country, that would use this gun and we also know that they each have a chip in their left ear. Roger, get that guy in Cancun up here, maybe he has some more keys"

"In the meantime keep tracking the shipments. I am now certain that each of the 3143 counties will have at least one storage facility, full of these boxes. That warehouse in Mexico is undoubtedly supplying all these items and I want contingency plans for blowing it off the face of the earth, in the next ten days, an industrial accident, of course.

Pete returned to his office and dialed a private number.

The phone was answered with the question, "What can I do for you Pete?"

"Chris, we need to meet as soon as possible. A secure, private location and Chris, it's urgent."

CHAPTER TWENTY-FIVE

From his roof-top veranda, Ka Kee watched the day end as a blanket of wet, cool fog started blanketing the city. He was smug at how well the operation was going. The gang of five were out in the country, and as of today, they were, collectively, averaging almost twenty-five contacts per day. The exact total was, as of an hour ago, almost four-hundred which eclipsed his 268, and brought the total to almost seven hundred. Running the sums in his head he figured that they were about a quarter of the way thru the 3143 so they would need another three months or so to finish the job.

In the penthouse, next door, Operation George, supervised by Susan and her crew, were charting the progress of the Gang of Five, and were amazed that Colonel Ping had already covered the sixteen counties in Maine as well as the fourteen counties in Vermont. The county commanders were now known in each venue and the list was growing rapidly. Major Yaning was still in Georgia, working the 159 counties in that state and the youngest, of the group, Major Wang Jianwu, was closing in on finishing up the eighty-seven counties in Minnesota and would then move to Wisconsin, but right now he was setting in a coffee shop, in St. Paul searching his soul, as he waited for the commander of Ramsy County to show.

He had tossed and turned all night trying to decide if the information he had received yesterday should be passed up the chain or if he should just let the sleeping dog lay.

It all started when the commander of Scott County, south of Minneapolis, had told him that he had heard that the storage facility in Coons Rapid, Anoka county had been robbed.

"Where did you hear this?" Wang had demanded.

The commander replied that his wife had been told by the commander of Anoka counties wife. He went on to explain that the wives were both members of a Chinese-American club in Minneapolis.

"When did this happen?"

"Apparently this past weekend."

Looking through his notes he asked, "Is the Anoka county commander Low Ming?"

"Yes, Sir."

Major Wang Jianwu consulted a small notebook and dialed a local number.

"Mr. Ming?"

"Yes."

"This is Wang Jianwu, an associate of Ka Kee. Please tell me what happened this weekend."

"Sir, the storage facility next to mine was full of electronic merchandise. It was robbed and several other units, including mine were broken into, but nothing is missing. The robbers opened several boxes but seeing only clothing they moved on to other units."

"Are you certain they did not take any of your boxes?"

"Yes, I am Sir."

"Thank you for the information, and Low, you do not need to report this up the chain. Understand?"

"Yes, Sir. Thank you, Sir."

As Wang was replacing his phone a Chinese gentlemen approached his table and asked, "Would you be an associate of Ka Kee?"

"Yes, my name is Wang Jianwu, please set down."

After the interview, as Wang was driving to his next appointment, he was still wrestling with his dilemma. Should he report the incident or just let it slide?

That night, after a Chinese dinner at a the China Star restaurant on Madison Avenue, in downtown Mankato, Minnesota, Wang was still perplexed, but finally duty won over and he picked up the phone and called his employer.

"Yes, Wang, Ka Kee here."

"Sir, I hope I am not bothering you at this late hour."

"No, its only five on the West coast."

"Oh, good." Continuing he added, "I ran into something today that concerns me. I don't know if it is important enough to concern you, but I felt I needed to make you aware of the situation."

"Of course Major, that is what I would expect from an officer of your caliper. So tell me, what concerns you?"

Wang detailed exactly what he knew about the robbery, how he had uncovered the information and finished by asking, "I hope it was right in bring you this information?"

"You did exactly the right thing Major. Continue your schedule and concern yourself, no more, with this subject. Understand?"

"Yes, Sir and thank you sir."

Ka Kee hung up the phone, his gut wrenching, and consulting his note book, dialed a number in Coons Rapids, Minnesota and a sleep voice answered, "Hello."

"Is this Ben Zaho?"

"Yes, who's calling please?"

"This is Ka Kee Leung, Ben."

Ben shook off the sleep, and replied with dreaded anticipation, "Yes, Sir, Yes, what can I do for you?"

"Was your storage unit robbed?"

Ben's heart sank and he stammered, "Yes, yes, it was Sir."

"Were any of the boxes stolen?"

"No, Sir. They thieves broke open two cartons but did not take anything."

"How many boxes were delivered to you?"

"296 Sir."

"Ben, I want to know, before the sun comes up, exactly how many boxes are in your storage unit, and Ben, if you lie to me you and every relative you have, will be dead by this time tomorrow."

The line went dead.

"Honey, who called?"

He could barely talk but managed to mumble, "Never mind dear, go back to sleep, I will be back in a couple of hours."

The dark green Range Rover flew to the storage unit. Ben finished counting the boxes, for the third time, set down on a folding chair, and starring at the ceiling asked, "Why me, why me, God." Tears streamed down his face and he threw-up the chicken dinner, he had eaten several hours earlier. The count was, of course, unanimous – two boxes were missing.

Before he could drag himself off the chair and lock-up his phone rang.

"Well?"

"Sir, two boxes are missing." Ben would have continued with the details about counting the inventory three times, but Ka Kee knew all he needed to know and the line went dead.

Ben just sat there, with visions of his dead grandchildren, racing through his head.

CHAPTER TWENTY-SIX

The e-mail to Jet was short and to the point.

Jet, I am fairly certain operation has been compromised. Two boxes missing from Minnesota storage unit in Anoka county. Need your input soonest.
KKL'

Ka Kee had been watching the news and there was no mention of the Chinese weather balloon, so that part of the operation was a success and by now the unit had to have made it's way across the country, and be out over the Atlantic.

In Washington, the FBI Chief, was perplexed when word came down the line that the President considered the balloon, just an accident, and choose to let the matter slide, so as not to increase tensions between the two countries. Chris wondered if the payments, that Hunter was reported to have received from China, had any bearing on the decision. He concluded that no one would ever know the truth except maybe Joe and Hunter.

The Chief's thinking was interrupted by his secretary on the intercom saying, "Sir, Pete Duncan is here to see you."

"Send him in."

Chris greeted Pete, as the old friends they were, and asked with great concern, "What's going on Pete?"

Pete collapsed on the big leather couch that looked out on the White house and said, "Wish I didn't have to share this, but circumstances leave me no choice. Chris, at this point I don't even know if your trustworthy, and its tearing me apart."

"Pete, you seriously have doubts about my trustworthiness? Really?"

"Yes, Chris. At this point, I don't know who to trust. I want to trust you, but what's happening is coming from that building," nodding his head at the White house, "and I am about as gun shy as a worn-out government employee can be, and Chris it's scary as hell."

Chris looked at his old friend and asked, "Is it the balloon thing?"

"That's the tip of the ice berg," Pete almost yelled and then added softly, "That's nothing compared to what I know."

"Pete, what do you know, tell me. I swear on my Mother's grave that I am not involved in any covert operations with the White house or anyone else.. I swear."

Pete looked around the office, and asked, "Chris, are we being recorded?"

Chris looked at his long time friend and with almost an acrimonious look and cocking his head said, "Friend, please remember who you are talking to. I took an oath to this country and I would not violate that trust for The President, The Attorney General or anyone else in this government. Am I crystal clear?"

"Crystal."

Pete stood up and walked over to the window and starring at the White house asked, "Who has the authority to authorize 6000 containers, from Mexico, to enter the United States, without inspection?"

Walking over to Chris and putting his nose inches from the Director's nose Pete repeated, in almost a whisper, "Who?"

Chris frowned, backed-up and said, "I don't think that could come from anyone, but the President.

"Bingo!" Pete almost yelled and then added, "You just earned a gold ribbon. Now, to earn another ribbon you need to tell me why the President would approve the importation of 3.6 million guns, 1.8 million Chinese Army uniforms and 1.8 million identity cards.

THE ARMY WITHIN ZHANLUE

Identity cards that can only be activated by passing the card within an inch of your ear lobe. Oh, not your ear and not mine but one of the 1.8 million people in country who have a computer chip, installed under the skin, on the back side of their left lobe."

Chris was dumb founded. He walked over to his friend, put his hands on his shoulders and asked, "Pete, are you OK?"

"OH!, So you think I have lost it and this is all just fiction of my imagination. Well here is the address of a storage unit on Vale street in Coon Rapids, Minnesota. There were 296 boxes there, filled with uniforms and guns and identification tags but I stole two of them and they are in my safe, at my office. I can also give you the address of several hundred more storage units from Maine to Georgia and everywhere in between that have similar inventories." Smiling at the Director he asked, "So what the hell do we do now, old friend?"

Chris looked at Pete, furrowed his brow and asked, "Why, why would the President approve the makings of a coup? Why?"

"Greed or a promised he could be King and Hunter would follow in his footsteps. There is no other reason. It's one of the two and it does not really make any difference the fact is it is happening and we have to stop it. Chris as we speak, twelve containers left Mexico today and twelve will leave tomorrow and the next day and next day etc. etc. etc."

"How many containers have shipped. The last time I checked the border station at Tecata the number was up to just over three-hundred."

"So", Chris observed, "Around five percent. Well that's not exactly nipping it the bud, but it could be worse."

"Chris, my people are drawing up plans to blow up the warehouse in Tecata."

"You can't do that, I can't do that, are you crazy?"

"Industrial accidents happen all the time. They are getting their natural gas from one of our pipelines that runs along the border. We could cut off the gas supply. They would soon complain and probable ask the Mayor of Tecata to get it fixed. We could send in a Spanish speaking technician that could install a devise that would let the building fill up with gas and then an explosive charge that would blow it sky high. I bet you have something in your labs that would fill the bill."

"So, we blow up the plant in Tecata, what then?"

"We raid the storage units, remove the goods and destroy them and then we start looking for ear lobes with computer chips and deport them, minus their chip, of course."

"Every building or airport scanning machine could be modified to expose a chip. Eventually we would catch most of them."

Chris asked, "Do you really think there are 1.8 million foreign agents in the country?"

"The Hill reported the other day that under Biden's watch 10.2 million illegals have entered the country since 2020. Could 1.8 of the 10.2 be agents? It's not outside the scope of reality. There are also 290,000 Chinese college students, in American colleges, and I would bet the farm a big majority, of them, are carrying chips around in their ears. Another point, why did this operation base in San Francisco?"

"I don't know," Chris acknowledged.

"It is the largest concentration of Chinese outside of Asia and the Chinese government just gave a Chinatown organization fifty million bucks to buy property on the edge of Chinatown."

"Pete, may I come to your office and see the boxes?"

"Sure, we can go now."

"Let's do it."

CHAPTER TWENTY-SEVEN

It was a quick ride to Pete's office and as he entered, the bull-pen of desks, on his way to his corner office, he yelled at Bill.

"Bill, bring the boxes to the secure conference room."

Chris followed Pete to the conference room, and within seconds, they were followed by Bill and a helper, each carrying a box.

"Help yourself, Chris."

The FBI Director pulled the nearest box across the desk, opened the cardboard flaps. The plastic sleeves with instructions and I.D. cards were on top. He slowly read the English side of the instructions, then picked up the I.D. cards and read the accompanying instruction sheet.

Carefully, he sat the two items aside and removed the three sets of khakis, which he piled next to the box, after giving the shoulder and arm patch insignia a quizzical look.

Below the clothing were two bubble wrapped items. The first bag contained an AK-47 look alike and within the packaging was an instructions sheet, in English and Chinese, on how to assemble the unit, and how to activate the chip in the handle, that would make the weapon operational.

Chris looked up at Pete and just shook his head before opening up the last package which held a 9mm hand gun.

It too had instructions on how to activate the I.D. Cards, and once activated, how to activate the weapon.

Chris noted that there was a small note at the bottom of the page that the recipient should purchase at least 500 rounds of standard 9mm ammunition.

With the box empty, the Director, turned and asked, "How many boxes were at the storage unit where you acquired these?"

"296," Bill replied.

"And how many storage units have you identified?"

"Well over 600, Sir" was Bill's answer.

"Can we assume that each storage unit contains about 300 boxes?"

"Yes, Sir."

"That's 18,000 boxes." Chris explained.

Bill interrupted and said, "Sir, you dropped a zero, it's 180,000 not 18K."

The director looked at Bill, cocked his head and said,"My mistake. You are absolutely correct. It is 180K." and then added, "so that means 360,000 fire arms, correct."

Bill nodded yes.

Following up Chris quickly said, "About twelve trucks cross the boarder every day, so that's 3600 boxes per day?"

Bill's one word reply was, "Bingo!" And then continuing Chris added, "That's 216,000 weapons per month."

The Director looking at Pete asked, "Can we go to your office, I need to set down."

The two men entered Pete's sanctuary and it was Chris's turn to plop down on the couch. In total disconsolateness he almost yelled at Pete, "Damn, Damn, Damn...how in the hell do we crack this nut?"

Pete replied, "I have been thinking about it and I think someone, at the White house got hoodwinked and it could not have been anyone but Joe or Hunter, and further I'll bet you the national debt that it was Hunter. Maybe some high ranking Mexican government official whispered in his ear that 'big bucks could be generated' if he (Hunter) would let a Mexican company import their dime store items with no duty."

Chris replied, "Wow, that's a far reach isn't it?"

"No, I don't think so. Look at the Fentanyl trade that Mexico and China have set up, through the Cartels. The Mexican Government has to be complicit and I think they were bribed by the Chinese. Want to bet that there is no one, in the Mexican government, that has ever been inside that Tecata warehouse? The security around it is awesome and all the employees are Chinese nationals and odds on are each one of them has an ear chip and further, they are all Chinese Army personnel, that will be dispersed into the country, after the last box has shipped. They will be 'The Army Within' commanders."

Chris nodded his head and observed, "I can't argue with the logic. The sixty-four-million-dollar question is what do we do now?"

"Chris we must stop the flow. We have to turn off the spigot. I am going to cut off the natural gas, yet today, and you need to find me a Spanish speaking technician that can install some kind of device that will let the building fill up with gas and then a trigger that can blow it to hell and back.

"Pete, you could go to jail for the rest of your life."

"True, but each one of those 360,000 guns could kill thirty Americans. Am I suppose to put my life and career above the lives of 10 million of my fellow countrymen?"

"Chris jumped off the couch and said, "I'm going back to the office and you, my good friend, shall have a Spanish speaking technician, ready to roll, in twenty-four hours. Good luck, my boy!"

The two men embraced and Chris shot out the door like a ball out of one of Grant's cannons.

CHAPTER TWENTY-EIGHT

Ka Kee's I-pad pinged. It was just about four am. and he was half-awake anyway, in that he had been tossing and turning all night. He sat on the edge of the bed, put his code number into the unit and brought up a secure E-mail. The message was from Jet and it was not his normal three liner.

> *'Student, have talked with only person that matters. Your situation fully understood. We recommend that you set tight for a week to ten days. If no threats materialize continue your operation. We remind you of Chinese Proverb: Success is not final, failure is not fatal: it is the courage to continue that counts.*
>
> *JHC'*

Ka Kee, laid back on the bed with his bare feet dangling over the side and smiled. He fondly remembered a proverb that his father had taught him when he was just a small boy. He recited it out loud, "To learn is to encounter one's own ignorance."

Wide awake he decided to brave the morning fog and cold. A brisk walk to the Gold Spike and back was just the ticket. Since the Spike was open 24/7, he knew Mr. Zavattero would have a cup of hot tea, for him to sip, before he turned around and headed back up Columbus street, for his temporary home.

His NTA tail, did not appreciate a walk up and down the foggy San Francisco hills at 5am, nor standing in a doorway across the street, from the Spike, freezing his butt off while 'Mr. Chip' sipped hot tea.

Back on the veranda, enjoying his American breakfast, Ka Kee picked up the phone and called Colonel He Ping.

"Yes General, what can I do for you?"

"Care to take a break for a few days?"

"Well, yes, I could, but that's not necessary. I'm scheduled to move into New Hampshire tomorrow and it only has ten counties, so it should go fast."

"He, take a break and go to Minnesota and hook up with Wang. I want you both to check out a potential problem in Coon Rapids, Minnesota. The commander of Anoka County is Ben Zaho, and I want you to look at his storage unit, which was broken into a few night's back. I don't trust his count and this is too important to ignore. Get back to me as soon as you have ferreted out the facts. Understand?"

"Yes, Sir. I'll pack my bag and head for the airport immediately. I'm in Burlington now, Sir, what city should I fly into in Minnesota?"

"Minneapolis, and have a safe trip."

"That Ping is one good man. Think I'll put him on my staff when this is over." he said out-loud, and in minutes the spooks across the street were relaying Colonel Ping's travel plans.

Next door, in the Holiday Inn Penthouse East Susan commented, to her assistant, with a big smile, "Sure is easier to tail them when they tell you where they are going, by the way, when will that bug in Chip's bedroom be active?"

"It's all set to be installed the next time he packs his bag and heads for the airport."

That came the next day, when Ka Kee headed for SFO at 6am. He was off to Denver, Cheyenne and Helena to meet with the county commanders, near all the U.S. military bases in the 'Big Sky' country, especially the one near the Air force Academy.

As the United flight cruised over the Rockies, preparing to land at the mile high Denver Airport, Ka Kee was struck by the landscape below him. Ridge after ridge of rugged mountains, all snow capped, for as far as you could see, from thirty thousand feet. No signs of man or civilization. This country was truly incredible, and he made up his mind that when this was all over he might have a home at the foot of these majestic mountains.

The Air Force Academy is home to over four-thousand cadets, and Ka Kee knew it would take a large contingent of his Army Within to neutralize that many fighting men. The academy was in El Paso county and the county commander, Fook Yan, was waiting for Ka Kee at the baggage claim area.

As they pulled out of the parking facility Ka Kee asked, "You are regular Army, correct?"

"Yes, Sir. I was the commanding officer at the Harbin Flight Academy in Heilongjiang Province."

"How long have you been in America?"

"I came across the border in 2022 and work as a gardener at the Air Force Academy so I have had access to the base for the last two years and Sir, I know every inch of the terrain. In addition, I have three co-workers that are also line officers. We will have over three hundred and fifty boots on the ground, on D-day, and should be able to neutralize the base within the opening hours."

"When you receive your consignment, alter your original plan that called for one large storage unit. Split the cargo up into small batches of about fifty boxes per unit."

Fook, took his eyes of the road, looked briefly at his leader and asked, "Is there a reason for that, Comrade General?"

Ka Kee smiled and said, "There is a Chinese Proverb that says, 'Don't concentrate all your prospects or resources in one thing or place, or you could loose everything.'"

"Yes, Sir. As you say Sir."

Ka Kee spent the rest of the day with Colonel Yan and was confident that this part of the operation would go like clock-work. As they were heading back for the Airport, Ka Kee asked, "Would you have time to do some work for me"?

Well I have two weeks vacation due, so yes. What did you have in mind?"

"There are sixty-four counties in Colorado. Would you be up to being the commander for the state and making sure that the sixty-four county commanders are all on the same page? In other words, that their storage facilities and manning plans are accurate and workable."

"I would be honored, Sir."

"Congratulations Colorado commander Yin, and by the way, your monthly allotment check will be increased by two-hundred percent starting the first of next month."

Setting in the United boarding area, with the sun setting behind the Rockies, waiting for his short hop to Cheyenne, Wyoming, Ka Kee congratulated himself on finding such a high caliper fellow traveler. Yin had just saved him days and days of travel and hopefully the commander of Larame County, Wyoming, might be of the same caliper. He really didn't relish traveling the twenty-three Wyoming counties that cover 93,000 square miles.

The trips into Wyoming and Montana had been eye openers for Ka Kee, but he couldn't wait for the United flight to fly through some fog, skim over the salt flats, and deposit him at SFO.

The lure of sea food was calling, and he vowed not to have another beef steak, for the rest of the year. You were not a real man, in Wyoming and Montana, unless you could choke down two pounds of blood-red-beef-meat and a liter of beer. He had been amazed to watch his country- men, eat like real cowboys, riding the range.

"Yes Pete, Susan said, "He is due into SFO any minute, and the bug is in place and Pete, our agent tailing him out of the Denver office, discovered that the El Paso county commander is a gardener at the Air Force Academy."

"Good work, Susan. If he heads for San Diego give me a code red heads up. Got it?"

"Sure Boss and thanks again for the kind words."

"You and your crew are doing a hell of a job."

Susan clicked off her phone and thought, "I wonder if Chip talks in his sleep?"

CHAPTER TWENTY-NINE

The natural gas flowing from the USA pipeline, into the warehouse in Tecata, had been shut off for almost twenty-four hours when Mayor Ruiz got an urgent call from General Lin Lau.

The gas-powered air conditioning system was down, and Lin Lau's maintenance people had determined that the natural gas supply had been interrupted.

"Mr. Mayor, can you find out what's going on? None of the air conditioners are working, and my people tell me it appears that the gas supply has been interrupted or shut off. Is that possible?"

"We have not heard about any interruptions here in Tecata and we use natural gas from the same line, so I don't think it's the line. It must be something broken or clogged up in your system. Would you like me to send a city technician out to check your system?"

"Yes, immediately, if possible, and thank you Mr. Mayor."

Sweating profusely, the Mayor hung up the phone and the FBI agent standing in front of his desk said, "We will take it from here, Mr. Mayor. Thank you for your cooperation, Sir."

"Si, Si" was all the mayor could choke out.

"And Mr. Mayor this meeting never happened and you never received a phone call from the warehouse. Si?"

"Si, Si, never happened, never happened Sir."

"And Mr. Mayor, the money you have in American banks will not be confiscated, you have my word. Oh, and that applies to the Swiss accounts as well."

The Mayor mopped his forehead with a big white handkerchief, and was so drained, he could not even get out of his chair, to show them out.

'Those damn Gringos. I hate them all. I really do hate them!' he thought as he managed, with great effort, to extract himself from the chair, walk across his office to a bar, and poured himself a water glass full of Patron Silver Tequila, which went down in one big gulp.

The panel truck, identified on the sides as a unit belonging to the City of Tecata, pulled up to the main gate of the huge warehouse south of Tecata and a smiling Mexican man said, "I'm from the Mayors office. Something wrong with your gas line I hear?"

A uniformed guard, wearing a sidearm, got into the passenger side, looked back into the truck to be sure there were no other occupants and motioned the driver through the double gates and up to the main entrance. "Do you speak English?"

"Some," the driver replied.

The guard jumped out, came around to the driver side, opened the door and said, "Let's go."

"I will need my tool bag, that's in the back."

The guard walked him to the rear of the vehicle where the driver, opened the back door, and reached in and picked up a large satchel and pointing to a box said, "I may need those parts as well."

The guard picked up the box, slammed the doors and said, "Follow me."

Inside the building the technician was greeted by the biggest Chinese man he had ever seen. Lin Lau said, "Follow me," and led the technician into the warehouse and indicated that he should get in the red golf cart.

The utility room was a quick ride, to about the middle of the building where the golf cart stopped, and Lin Lau asked, "You live in Tecata?"

"Si. My brother-in-law is Mayor Ruiz."

"Well, please thank the Major for sending you so quickly. Do you need any help?"

"No, Senior, it's probably just a malfunction valve and I have several spares so I'm sure I can get it back up and running in no time."

"Do you need any assistance?"

"No, but thank you for the offer."

"When you are finished just honk the golf cart horn and either I or one of my staff will take you back to the entrance.

"Thank you, Sir."

The utility room was well configured and Special Agent Andrew Gomez had no trouble locating the incoming gas line. Forty-five minutes later, a shinny new gas control valve was in place and operational. Andrew reached down in his bag and removed a paging type device, keyed in a six digit code, and the technicians working, at the gas line control center, across the border from Tecata, turned the gas back on.

Andrew waited five minutes and then bleed the air out of the line until the smell of the natural gas reached his nose. At that point, he double checked that all the units were functioning properly, and tapping a new component, he had added to the line, he thought, 'Glad I will be fifty miles away when this baby goes.'

He gathered up his tools and the 'defective-value' he had replaced, and deposited them in the golf cart and then pushed the horn button.

A hundred feet away a man walked out into the isle, saw the technician standing by the golf cart and started jogging his way.

"How did it go?"

"Just fine, replaced this valve, pointing to the box, and everything is back up and on line."

"What do I owe you, son?"

"No charge, Sir. My brother-in-law, the Mayor, would be unhappy with me if I charge you."

Lin Lau reached in his pocket, peeled off three one-hundred-dollar bills, and stuffed them in Andrew's shirt pocket saying, "What the

Mayor does not know won't hurt him." and with a wink, continued, "Hop in and I'll take you back to the office."

"Thank you, Sir."

As Andrew drove back to the border, a call came in from Pete. "Well, how did it go Andy?"

"Looking at his watch, he replied, "You might want to set your watch for about fifteen hours from now. It's going to be one hell of a bang, and boss, they didn't have a clue and on top of that I got a three-hundred-dollar tip."

Laughing Pete said, "Will we see that on your income tax form Andy?" And then continuing, "Well done Son, and by the way have you ever been to Mexico?"

"Yes, Sir I have. Went down to Cabo when I was in college, at San Diego State, put haven't been back since."

"Well you should go down there sometime. I hear the beaches are incredible."

"Thanks for the advice. Sir."

CHAPTER THIRTY

Ka Kee had been avoiding contact with the CEO of the battery plant in Illinois, Lin Wong, and the ultimate commander of the 'Army Within', for two reasons, both of which now seemed mute.

Number one, there had been no need to keep him in the loop, on the progress of stocking the storage units around the country, as the operation was proceeding as planned.

Secondly, since there was an obvious clash of personalities, less contact would avoid the chance of some kind of irreparable breach taking place, that could jeopardize the entire operation.

He had been over it a hundred times and Ka Kee knew he could no longer procrastinate. He had to tell Wong of the possible compromise.

Reading the e-mail for the tenth time, having tweaked it, at least that often, he was now reading, what he hoped was the final draft.

> *'Lin Wong,*
> *The project may have been compromised. I have advised JHC and he as advised the one who needs to know. <u>They</u> advise me to set tight and continue the operation. You may wish to develop contingency plan for emergency exit. Do not think you can be tied to my operation but could be wrong.*
> *KKL'*

Ka Kee hit the send button as he was thinking, 'I wonder how Comrade Wong will react to this news?'

The reaction the e-mail generated was not even on Ka Kee's radar.

Upon reading the e-mail form Ka Kee, Lin Wong picked up his phone and demanded that his second in charge come to his office immediately.

Within minutes his second in command, was standing in front of his boss and Lin was saying, "Ho, I have a family emergency and must return home immediately. I will be gone for at least two weeks. You are in charge. If you have any urgent problems you may discuss them with Ka Kee in San Francisco. Understood?"

"Yes, Sir, understood."

"You are dismissed."

Lin finished filling his briefcase with sensitive documents, drove to the Holiday Inn, packed his bag and headed for O'hare.

The Lufthansa flight was just over eight hours and Lin was tired but a sense of relief was coursing through his veins as he claimed his luggage and headed for customs at the Munich airport.

The four-hour train ride from Munich to Zurich, Switzerland was incredibly beautiful and Lin Wong's visit with the USC Group AG bank satisfied his every doubt. The four million US dollars, his kickback on the battery plant project, was safe and sound.

At the Radisson Blu hotel, in downtown Zurich, he sent an e-mail to his wife and gave her instructions for meeting him. He then went downstairs to the hotel maintenance department, located the supervisor, determined the hotel did have an industrial shredder, gave the supervisor a 100 Euro bill and watched his I-pad and phone get chewed into little pieces.

Ho Huing, Lin Wong's second in command, was the officer that President Hu was paying, to make sure Lin did not get too big for his britches.

Three days after Lin left the office, leaving Ho in charge, Ka Kee made a call to Lin, and was informed that Mr. Wong had taken emergency leave and that Mr. Huing was the acting manager.

"Let me speak to Mr. Huing please."

"Ho Hing here."

"Ho, Ka Kee Leung in San Francisco. How are you today?"

"Just fine Sir, nice to talk with you again."

"Ho, where is Comrade Wong?"

"Sir, I assume he is in transit to his home in Guangdong provenience Sir. He had a family emergency."

"When did he leave?"

"The last time I saw him was Tuesday morning so he has been gone three days, Sir. Is there a problem?"

"No, no problem. Thank you for the information." The line went dead and Ho had a feeling in his gut that Comrade Wong might just be history.

The e-mail to Jet was short and sweet.

Three days later Jet reported.

> 'Lin Wong's wife arrested as she was departing for Europe. You are now in charge of all USA operations and that appointment comes from the top. Illinois operation has been advised. Congratulations, Student.
> JHC'

CHAPTER THIRTY-ONE

It had been fourteen hours and thirty-three minutes since Agent Andrew Gomez had driven away from the warehouse in Tecata.
About an hour ago the warehouse had started filling up with natural gas and those sleeping, in the makeshift dormitory did not awake. The night shift workers finally noticed the strange odor and the officer in charge sent one of his junior officers to investigate.

The junior officer took the red golf cart to the utility area. Climbed out, opened the utility room door and was instantly dust.

The roof of the huge building lifted up a good twenty feet, above its original height, all four walls fell outward and the roof crushed down leaving a debris pile no higher than eight feet.

A cloud of dust rose up, like an atom bombs mushroom cloud, and the prevailing winds dispersed it towards Yuma.

Even though the boarder station was two miles away, every window was blown out and several agents were nursing flying glass cuts.

The residents of Tecata were tossed out of their beds and many sub-standard buildings lost roofs or were completely blown down. No one was killed in the city, but at the warehouse they would be digging bodies out of the wreckage for the next few years, provided the Mexican government decided the effort, to clean up the site, was worth while.

The explosion was national news and Ka Kee, watched the reporting as he hastily packed his bag. Before departing his home, away from home, for the last time, he e-mailed the his five associates, and told them:

> *'Disband operations. Make your way to Mexico City office.*
>
> *KKL'*

Looking around the penthouse for the last time Ka Kee smiled and thought. 'Jet will be disappointed with his student.'

When he opened the suite door, to take the elevator, Susan Loveless and six agents, guns drawn, greeted him, and none were smiling.

The attractive lady said, "General Ka Kee Leung, you are under arrest. Formal charges will be made at your arrangement. As she was talking one of the agents removed Ka Kee's lap top from his briefcase and said, "Sir, may I have your cell phone."

Ka Kee reached into his breast pocket and handed the unit to the agent while palming a small red capsule.

On the ride to the lobby he coughed, put his hand up to his mouth and bit down hard on the capsule.

There were no press reports of the death, of a Chinese national, who had been visiting friends in San Francisco, other than an official note to the Chinese Embassy, on Laguna street, asking for instructions for the disposal of the body.

As Jet sat on his patio, taking in the ever changing ocean view he knew that his student was with his ancestors. Jet was sad, he had loved the boy, like the son he never had and the loss made him realize he was just too old. He needed to put his former life, in a small boat, take it down to the islands beach, and watch it sail away.

Reminded of an old Chinese proverb he recited it from memory.

'A journey of a thousand miles begins with a single step'

Lights went off in his head and he stood up, walked to the edge of the patio, looked up and said, "Ka Kee, It feels like you left, with a piece of my heart."

CHAPTER THIRTY-TWO

The meeting between the FBI Director, the Director of the National Threat Assessment Center and the President's son had been delicately arranged by the Attorney General himself.

It took place in the FBI Directors office at 3pm Eastern standard time, one week to the day since Ka Kee's demise.

After introductions around Pete picked up the ball and said, "First, thank you for granting this interview. Our only reason, for this meeting, is to understand why the President approved the importation of 6000 containers, from Mexico, without the units being subjected to the normal boarder inspection protocol."

Chris and Pete smiled at their guest and waited for his explanation.

The middle-aged man looked off into space, frowned and then said, "Yes, as I recall we, the family, were having a private dinner with the President of Mexico and after dinner the President and I were talking. He told me about his son-in-law that had invested millions in a general hardware business, which I assumed to be something like Ace Hardware. At any rate long story short the factory overproduced hundreds of thousands of items and the President wondered if they could import the items with no duty or inspection."

Chris asked, "And what was your response?"

"I told him it was possible and later I mentioned it to some of Dad's staff and it kind of snow-balled form there."

"So as far as you knew the containers would be full of cheap hardware items that would get sold around America."

"That's correct."

"Did the President of Mexico compensate you in any way for your help?"

"Well not directly but I understand the DNC received a generous donation for Dad's re-election campaign."

Chris looked at Pete, they both put on a resignation look and Chris said, "Well, thank you for your clarification. I don't think we will need to look into this any further."

"You are welcome, glad to be of service." and with that said, he exited the office and his secret service detail, followed down to the waiting limousine.

Chris looked at Pete and said, "Well, do you buy it?"

"Of course, and I also believe in the tooth fairy."

APPENDIX

President Hu -	Like to operate out of his underground bunker and is still China's CEO.
Joseph Robinette Biden Jr. -	President of United States.
Jet how Cheung -	Lives on Bai'am Island off the coast of China, with his sister-in-law and is looking forward to raiding Taiwan's Museum.
First Class Colonel General Ka Kee Leung -	Died in San Francisco. Ashes in Yunnan Province.
General Lin Wong -	CEO of Illinois battery plant and selected to run America after coup. Died in Europe.
Captain Dan Lee -	Chinese Army officer, defected.
Frank Woo -	Commander of Kankakee county, Illinois.
P.K. Fong -	Jefferson county commander, Kentucky.
Mayor Ruiz -	Mayor of Tecata, Mexico
General Lin Lou -	In Charge of Tecata warehouse
Wuhan -	Chairman Gang of Eight – San Francisco
Wo Hoing -	Chinese government banking official
Mike Armacost -	Bank of America executive, San Francisco
Don Zavattero -	Owner Gold Spike, San Francisco
My Ling -	Granddaughter of Chairman Wuhan
Fook So -	Aroostook County commander

John Hammond -	Special Agent – National Threat Assessment Center.
Peter M. Duncan -	Chief of NTA
Roger Pierce -	Special Agent – NTA
Susan Loveless -	Special Agent – NTA
Chris -	FBI Director
Bill -	Peter Duncan assistant
Colonel He Ping -	Ka Kee assistant
Major Wang Jainwu -	Ka Kee assistant
Major Yang Xuejun -	Ka Kee assistant
Major Zhang Youxia -	Ka Kee assistant
Major Zhou Yaning -	Ka Kee assistant
Terry Pinzon -	Special Agent – NTA
Low Min -	Commander Ramsy County, Minnesota
Ben Zaho -	Commander Anoka County- Minnesota
Fook Yin -	Commander El Paso County, Colorado State
Andrew Gomez -	Special Explosive agent – NTA
Hunter -	Second Officer – Illinois battery plant. President Biden's Son

OTHER BOOKS BY JACK D. WAGGONER

- BIRDNEST
- FLIGHT TO PUSKA
- THE RAINBOW ZHANLUE (Strategy)
- THE VOYAGES UNDER ARCTURUS
- KILLING ISIS
- GOD'S PARALLEL PLANETS
- DRAGON BREATH ZHANLUE (Strategy)

www.ingramcontent.com/pod-product-compliance
Lightning Source LLC
LaVergne TN
LVHW050810181224
799395LV00001B/164